BLACKOUT
ODYSSEY

a novel

VICTORIA FEISTNER

Milton, Ontario

This is a work of fiction. All of the characters, events, and organizations portrayed in this novel are either products of the author's imagination or are used fictitiously.

Brain Lag
Milton, Ontario
http://www.brain-lag.com/

Cover artwork by Victoria Feistner

ISBN 978-1-928011-52-1

Library and Archives Canada Cataloguing in Publication

Title: Blackout odyssey : a novel / Victoria Feistner.
Names: Feistner, Victoria, author.
Identifiers: Canadiana (print) 20210200901 | Canadiana (ebook) 20210200928 | ISBN 9781928011521
    (softcover) | ISBN 9781928011538 (ebook)
Classification: LCC PS8611.E453 B53 2021 | DDC C813/.6—dc23

For Lilithe,
who always uses her words

PROLOGUE

Mallory had never seen the stars like this before in Toronto. When camping as a kid, she'd been amazed at the ribbons of galaxy she'd seen through the trees while listening to the whispering and shushing leaves—the music of an August night in the country. This was different: cars rolled by, people talked and laughed, dogs barked and babies cried. And yet the dome of stars over the plaza shone as bright and clear as any camp-night. The dewy grass was chilly, then refreshing, under her dragging and cut-up feet. A blessed numbness crept after the chill until she sighed with relief. She debated throwing her remaining shoe away but tucked in its toes was her Nokia; the long heel of her black leather pump made a better grip for her weary fingers.

High overhead, the moon guided her along a path. Did its height mean it was early or late? She didn't know. She'd never needed to, before... The digital signage on the corner of Mel Lastman Square was dark, its clock with it.

Someone played a guitar. Not too badly, either.

A smell from those camping days drifted over, a memory long buried and rarely revisited: naphtha.

She peered this way and that, discerning movement in the night but not shapes until a *hiss* from her left—as a tiny Coleman lantern flared into life—illuminated a picnic table and a small family. A woman bent over a cooler, pulling out items. Two children draped over the pine panels as only adolescents, dead from boredom, could. The younger boy leaned hopefully into the Coleman's feeble light, straining to see his old, beaten-up Game Boy's screen.

"Turn that thing off," snapped the man, still fiddling with the camp-stove. Then: "See? I told you this old stuff would still work."

"Our dad says that you're a bum and you should get your own garage," the older girl declared.

The man straightened. "Yeah, well, your dad owes me garage space. He knows why. Anyway. Behold! I have brought you fire!"

"Can you bring us some hot water?" the woman asked. She seemed to take notice of Mallory, her eyes large in the darkness. "You okay, honey?"

Mallory snapped out of her trance, realizing she'd been staring. "Sorry! Sorry for—" Staring? Bothering you? Intruding? All things she would say on a regular day. But today was not regular.

The woman smiled and patted the bench. She was achingly beautiful, and despite the late hour and the insanity, well-put together and clean in a way that only reinforced Mallory's grime, torn outfit, and missing shoe(s).

Normally nothing could induce her to sit with strangers like this. But she stepped forward, walking on the outside of her feet to keep the open blisters clear off the ground.

"You look like you've had a rough time," the beautiful woman said. "Hell of a day, huh?"

"Yeah." Nervous at first, but as Mallory sat, the tension drained out of her until she too slumped like a teenager, her shoe and phone in her lap.

"I'm still hot," whined the boy, while the older girl regarded their new guest with undisguised disdain.

"When I was a boy, that's what August *was*," said the man, cheerfully. "Hot. And there was nothing you could do about it. Just be hot."

"Yeah, but that's because you're, like, *ancient*, Uncle Daniel." The girl continued to stare at Mallory. "And your air-conditioning was, like, sitting in a pond."

"Don't knock the pond," he replied, busy with the stove.

"Mom, do we have to stay here?" the boy asked.

The beautiful woman reached over to ruffle her son's dark hair, leaving it in curly disarray. "I told you to bring a book."

"This is the worst," the girl declared, while across the square families spread blankets and opened their own coolers, escaping the built-up heat of their apartments, hoping to gain relief, and wondering at the strangeness of the day. Laughter danced upwards like the sparks from the tiny camping stove. The guitar played out in the unseeable night, its notes bouncing off the buildings that ringed the plaza.

"The worst," Mallory agreed under her breath, so tired her bones ached, as though she was made of lead, a heavy broken weight on bare feet. A hiss of steam escaped the kettle and the beautiful woman passed the man a canister. As he unscrewed the lid, the odour wound its way around Mallory like a gentle nudging hand, pulling her upright.

He noted her attention. "Want some coffee?"

"Please." It escaped from Mallory's lips before she could stop it. She should leave; she still had a long way to go and someone waiting, no doubt worried. Her cell phone felt warm under her clenched fingers. The pair of adults both laughed, wearing open expressions, curiosity and friendliness, and when Mallory opened her mouth to protest and apologize, what squeaked out instead was: "Yes, please."

The man's smile broadened. "Always happy to share a good cup of coffee." He glanced at the smelly campstove and his lips twitched. "Well, this won't be *good*, but it'll be hot and caffeinated, anyway. How do you take it, Ms...?"

"Mallory. Mallory Doran. Cream and sugar, please."

"We don't have either of those," the woman said, her own smile like the shining moon through the trees. "But it's hot?"

"Sounds perfect." Mallory meant it.

"Ugh," groaned the girl.

"Behave yourself," her mother chided. Then to Mallory: "You can call me Shelly. This is my brother, Daniel Gabriel, and my two children Dawn and Dee."

"Nice to meet you." Mallory was aware she was mumbling, embarrassed, as she accepted the proffered yellowed melamine cup with deep and humbled gratitude. She wrapped chilled fingers around it, nearly at tears from the warmth, and light, and kindness, and tried to seem more human. "What a day, eh?"

"What a day indeed." Daniel Gabriel, the coffee seen to, settled into the picnic table bench, draping an arm around his niece's shoulders while she squirmed away. "We live—Shelly and the kids live—not too far away. So it was simple enough to set up out here to eat, away from the stuffy house."

Shelly nodded in agreement, making sandwiches

from supplies in the cooler.

"But you look like you've been walking a lot," Daniel Gabriel continued, his eyes suddenly very blue in the low light, and Mallory couldn't look away. "Why don't you tell us about your day while we eat?"

They all looked at her, their gazes like limelight, hot and unyielding. Even Dee had put away his Game Boy. A moth fluttered and bumped into the lantern, confused. Shelly reached out to urge it away, gently, until it saw the moon again and flew off.

"I... don't know where to start." Mallory's voice cracked, and she bent her head to sip coffee, still acutely aware of all the attention on her. Even the guitarist had paused.

Shelly handed her a sandwich, her smile inviting. "Just start at the beginning, hon. We're not going anywhere."

PART ONE

1.
A LONG NIGHT'S DAY

I rested my head against the metal rim of the open window. The thick air only gusted in when the bus moved, and when in rare motion, the vehicle joggled so that my head gently bumped along with it.

I checked my watch again: 3:55 p.m.

"Traffic shouldn't be this bad, should it?" I asked Aggie, on my left.

Aggie peered up from her stack of presentation papers, blinking behind her round glasses. After taking a moment to gain her bearings, she shrugged. "I don't know this part of the city."

"I don't either." I wasn't sure we were even in Toronto proper yet. Someone at the front of the bus started playing music without headphones on; the CD Walkman skipped, adding even further insult to the tinny sounds of 'Unchained Melody'. I sighed and rested my temple against the warm glass. Outside, the air shimmered over the tops of the cars, the August sun still high in the sky.

Whenever I shifted in the seat, the vinyl of the ancient bus stuck to the backs of my thighs, my skirt having ridden up; between the oversized presentation case resting on my feet, my purse in my lap, and Aggie next to me, I had little room. I furtively managed a shimmy to yank the fabric of my skirt down enough to create a barrier.

"Could be worse," Aggie murmured, highlighter dragging across the page. "At least we're not in three-piece suits."

Suit skirt, jacket, and tights was bad enough. "The people in those suits don't have to take transit. They have drivers. Or can afford a cab, anyway."

Aggie gave a *hmm* of agreement, a sort of 'true, but what can you do?' noise. The scritch of her highlighter and the tinny, skipping saxophone music skittered like tiny nails against my skin under the layers of business wear. Acutely aware of sweat trapped between my shoulder blades, I shifted against the hard back of the seat, hoping to fend it off before it became a true itch I wouldn't be able to scratch.

Cold showers. Cold drinks on a patio. Ice cream. Ice floes. Air-con turned so high you can smell the hole in the ozone layer.

Meditation didn't help. I checked my watch: 3:57. "Do you think they'll expect us back in the office?"

Aggie shook her head, some of her hair escaping her bun. "I spoke to John as we were heading out." She straightened, capping her highlighter, and scratched at her nose. "He said we might as well just go home. By the time we get to Lawrence West it'll be close to 5:00 anyway."

"He probably just wants to leave early too."

"He's heading in the opposite direction." Aggie pulled out her elastic and redid her bun, her black hair smooth under her hands. "Taking tomorrow off. Cottage."

"Lucky." I fought the urge to check my watch again. Maybe I should have brought work to look over too but the presentation case holding our movie-poster-sized display boards was heavy and awkward enough. My tiny purse had barely enough space for my wallet, keys, cell phone, and makeup. The bus lurched forward as whatever held up traffic finally eased.

Aggie was back at her presentation notes. I couldn't read on a bus, anyway. Especially one so herky-jerky; I'd be sick. That's why I was by the window. Ahead of us, the ass with the CD player had moved on to louder, more obnoxious musical choices, attracting the attention and ire of people around him. "Is it okay with you if I make a call?"

My colleague blinked at me. She looked like an owl when she did that, blinking before answering any question; worse when she had her reading glasses on, those ancient 90s round-frame monstrosities that she'd worn since high school. At least during the presentation she didn't need them; I doubt the folks at the Darlington Nuclear Power Plant would have taken her at all seriously. Or maybe they wouldn't have noticed—after all, most of them were engineers and seriously nerdy themselves. "What?"

I fished my cell phone out of my tiny purse. "Do you mind? I'll be quick."

"Oh, right." Aggie didn't have a cell phone of her own, she refused to spend the money on one. Work reimbursed us the bills anyway, so what difference did it make? Mind you, I'd fork out for new glasses too. Aggie and I disagreed on many monetary issues.

I spent a moment admiring the little Nokia's boxy heft. John had talked a lot about the advantages of this model over the others, but since I didn't want to admit it was my first cell phone and I had no idea what he was talking about, I merely made thoughtful noises. In the end he didn't want my opinion anyway; he just wanted to talk specs at someone. (Some days it seemed like half of my job description was letting managers—who always sat with one leg on my desk, instead of pulling up a chair like a normal human—talk in my direction while I made appreciative noises. It drove some other girls in the office crazy, but I've practised a very good listening face while I continue thinking about my own work. After a while, listening to my managers was like meditation or staring out a window. Restful.)

I had a bar of signal and two bars of battery. I wish it was a percentage or a number—how long would two bars last me?—but as ever the Nokia supplied no answers, only questions. Still, it had Snake to play. Could I play Snake on a moving vehicle? With at least an hour of subway transit still to go, better not to chance the nausea.

A quick side-eye to Aggie to make sure she was still absorbed in her work, then I dialed Dylan, the number well-practised.

"Hello?"

"Hi." I kept my voice down. "It's me."

"Hello? Who is this?"

"It's me, Mallory."

"Oh, hey, babe. Back at the office already?"

"No, still on the bus. Heading to Scarborough Town Centre. John said we could just go home."

"Oh, great! So you'll be home early. You can put your feet up while I finish dinner."

I giggled. I did very much enjoy watching Dylan cook; he acted like one of those chefs on TV, all towels flipped over his shoulder and one-handed tossing of sizzling frying pans. He had a gas stove, too. No one I knew who was our age had a gas stove. It felt very fancy. "What are you making?"

Silence, leaving me with just a crackle of static and overheard tinny reggae. Then: "It's a surprise."

A surprise? "What? Why? What does that mean? Is it lobster? Why do you keep trying to get me to eat lobster?"

Dylan laughed. "It's not lobster, don't worry, I've learned my lesson. It's a surprise because it's a special occasion–just a second, the door–" He put the phone down on the counter. With the receiver pressed against my ear I could just about hear him talking in Spanish with a squeaky female voice replying. "Sorry about that. Camila needed to borrow a lemon."

I made a face. Camila was always borrowing something. Didn't she ever grocery shop? Dylan always laughed off my narrowed-eye suspicion claiming he was being neighbourly, and anyway, she always paid him back. He laughed a lot. It was one of the things I loved about him. "What surprise?" I prompted, eager to move on from our neighbour.

That laugh. "You'll find out tonight. I'm not telling you anything–shit, I gotta take something out of the oven–"

I pulled my ear away to examine the black and beige screen. Apparently I'd used up a bar of battery already? How? "I should go anyway, babe. Do you need me to pick up anything?"

"Actually, yes." His voice sounded muffled, and I imagined he had the phone receiver tucked under his chin. "Can you–shit, I gotta deal with this. Give me a call in a few, okay?"

"I'll call you from the station, we should be there soon–"

"Great," came the still-muffled reply, then sounds of clattering and swearing. "Gotta go!"

"Okay, love y—" Dial tone. I pulled away the cell phone and checked the battery again. Still one bar. Why did these make no sense? The bus hit a bump or a pothole and the little Nokia jumped out of my hands; I scrabbled to catch it.

Aggie watched me from the corner of her eyes. "You're not supposed to use that for personal calls."

"It was an emergency."

"No it wasn't."

"Yes it was."

She rolled her eyes and went back to her presentation, having moved on from highlighting to scribbled notes with a red pen. She went into each presentation with copious notes from the last tweaking right until go-time, but once we were in the room she stayed on script. Whereas I liked to improvise and go with the flow. Through trial and error we'd learned that the most effective combination was to have her present the first half and me on the second so I could answer questions as they appeared. "So what's the surprise?"

"What?"

"You mentioned a surprise. So what is it?"

"Well, I don't know, because it's a surprise. He said it's for a special occasion." I stuffed the cell phone into my jacket pocket. It strained the seams but would remind me to make the call before I got on the subway.

Aggie looked up from her papers. "What's the special occasion?"

I mulled it over. "I guess our anniversary is coming up... but it's two weeks from now."

She made a little O with her lips. "Maybe it's that? Aren't you away next weekend for that 'Women In STEM' conference?"

"Yeah, and then he's away with his brothers for a

camping trip..." I tapped my finger against my nose. "That's probably it then."

"Fancy. How many years?"

"Three."

Aggie made the O again, but this time she kept staring at me until I squirmed.

"What?"

"Three years? And he's bumping up your anniversary dinner by two weeks?"

I gave a slight shrug. "We're not really anniversary people. Like, last year we both forgot. I'm surprised he's bothering."

"Yeah, but it's *three*." Aggie paused to let the bus driver make an announcement, something about possible disruptions at the station. "Three-year anniversaries. You know what that means."

"Uh. Paper? I think? I don't know. Copper?"

"No, I mean–!" She rolled her eyes again, while starting to pack up. "C'mon, Mal, isn't it obvious? It's a 'special occasion' dinner."

"Yeah, our anniversary."

She sighed, snapping her binder shut. "I can't believe it's *me* spelling this out for *you*: he's going to propose. That's what he means by 'special occasion'."

I stared at her for a long moment as pieces flew together. Having a special dinner two weeks before our anniversary; that weird shopping trip that his brother came into town for last month that I was told was too boring for me to accompany them; phone calls that stopped when I walked into the room. All the extra groceries he's been laying in. Him booking two days off work as a 'staycation'. "Oh my god."

Aggie grinned. "Try to look surprised when you walk in the door." She squinted.

"Did you just wink at me?"

"Yes." She squinted again.

"You wink with one eye, you know that, right?"

She smacked me with her binder, and we both laughed.

I felt a little giddy, like I could open the window and fly away, as the bus pulled into the loop at Scarborough Town Centre Station. I'd been looking forward to dinner anyway—Dylan is a great cook, he learned from both his Peruvian *abuela* and his Irish mother; he really doesn't appreciate potato jokes—but now I was especially excited and did a little stamp of my feet while I waited my turn in line to disembark. Aggie was probably right. I mean, three years in is usually 'shit or get off the pot' time, isn't it? And our anniversary *was* coming up.

I tried to manoeuvre the large presentation case off the bus without hitting anyone. Outside, the heat was even worse, even in the shaded terminal; sunlight reflecting off the acres of asphalt surroundings caused the air to ripple and the humidity made me gasp. The inside of the station *might* be cooler, or it might be like inside an oven; although at least ovens generally had fans. The Scarborough Rapid Transit cars were often packed enough that the gasping air-conditioning did nothing. Probably no relief until Kennedy.

There were a lot of people gathered on the lower level by the bus stops. No one flowed away from the parked vehicles and up the escalators to the overhead light rail. Some people got on the bus I'd just left behind, but most milled around by the station entrance.

"What's all this?" Aggie asked, by my shoulder, carrying her own armload of presentation binders and other materials. Since she's quite a bit shorter than I am—and I'm not very tall—the jostling of the crowd meant she was being shoved a lot. I wiggled us to the periphery. "Didn't the driver say something about a power outage?"

"Maybe?" I hadn't been listening. Even in my heels I couldn't see past the heads of the crowds. Standing on my tiptoes didn't improve things. "Fuck. If there's a power outage here, do you think the whole SRT's down?"

"Probably not," Aggie replied. "Probably just the station." She gave me her armload of stuff—I had to juggle but managed—and disappeared through the crowd to where a TTC employee was trying to issue directions. After a few sweaty minutes she reappeared dodging someone's elbow to take back her materials. "It's not just the tracks. The whole station doesn't have power. Neither does McCowan Station next door."

"What about the rest of the TTC?"

"He doesn't know."

"Fuck."

Aggie gave a heavy sigh while adjusting her armful. "They're organizing shuttle buses."

I groaned. Shuttle buses, in August heat, crammed full of people, on routes that were already full of cars—always a nightmare. "I hate the east end."

"It's not the east end's fault." She shifted again. "It's probably only to Kennedy anyway. How long could that take?"

I groaned again. Visions of being home early and enjoying a cold drink disappeared. Miles to go before I slept, and all that. "Easy for you to say, you're only going to Don Mills. I'm going all the way to Etobicoke." Clear across the city, in rush hour.

Aggie lifted her shoulders and let them drop. "You

either get on a shuttle now or wait to see if they get the power back on."

I sighed. "Where did he say the shuttle buses would be?"

She pointed to the far end of the station. Of course.

I went first, Aggie close behind; the large presentation case served as a make-shift icebreaker, urging people out of our way. Any dodging I did saved her the effort. When I stopped, she bumped into my shoulders. "Sorry." The crowd had grown thicker, more agitated; someone shoved into my side, accidentally, and my purse strained at its skinny strap. I hefted it closer to me, but I needed my hands for the presentation case.

Voices in a melange of languages and accents flowed around us, most sounding as tired and sweaty as I was. My feet were already sore after a day in heels and now I'd probably be standing at least to Kennedy, if not the entire way to Islington. *Suck it up, buttercup.* I squared my shoulders and pressed on, but the crowd had the same problems I did. "Excuse me," I said, over and over, politely, but there wasn't space to give.

"Someone just said the whole TTC's down," someone remarked to their neighbour, loud enough to overhear.

"I just heard that the whole *city's* down," someone else replied, and with that, the crowd broke out into a babble of questions.

"Did you hear that?"

"Maybe the fare guy knows what's going on."

"Why would they know?"

"They've got phones, don't they?"

Phones. *Shit.* I'd told Dylan I'd phone him back, and given that I was now going to be late—I twisted around to find Aggie. "I need to find a phone."

2.
REVERSE CHARGES

"What? Now?" Aggie stared up at me and then back towards the crowd. Another bus pulled up and people surged towards it. "Call him from Kennedy."

It's hindsight that makes me wish I'd agreed with her. "I might as well call him now... Who knows, maybe by the time I'm done, the SRT will be back up and running? These brown-outs usually don't last that long."

Aggie answered with a frown of doubt, but then shrugged; my choice to make, after all. She waved goodbye, and I waved good luck back to her as she disappeared onto a sardine-can-turned Don Mills bus. But at least she was on a regular service vehicle and she'd be dropped off near her home.

Adjusting the straps on my presentation case, I turned back towards the entrance, against the crowd. Around me, people grew more convinced of bigger problems than a station power outage.

"Look at the lights in the mall sign—the sign's off."

"Look at the traffic lights!"

"The whole fucking neighbourhood must be down."

Surprise surged and receded like waves on a beach. It was Scarborough, after all. Brownouts happened in the summer, especially in a heat wave, when everyone turned on their air-conditioners at once. And the SRT—the SRT was always failing for one reason or another.

Someone caught my shoulder in their rush to make one of the shuttle buses, and the momentum and the presentation case spun me around, twisting one of my ankles too far. Down I went with a shriek of surprise, my purse and case slipping off my shoulder, scattering make-up and give-away pens everywhere. To the guy's credit, he swooped back to apologize instantly and to help me up—but I was fine, just caught off guard. I waved him away to catch the bus and he thanked me and dashed back into the throng.

I stayed on the floor gathering up the spill and stuffing it all back wherever it would fit—I'd sort it out at home. My ankle didn't even hurt much, just a throb, already disappearing. "No harm, no foul," I muttered, wiggling my toes before replacing my black pump.

The phones were inside the glass enclosure, next to the escalators. One bank had a hastily-scrawled "out of order" sign taped to them, and yellow caution tape wound around. The other bank of three was in service, but appeared to have line-ups five people deep for each.

I brushed sweating bangs out of my face and craned around, taking stock of the surroundings. The lower concourse was a crush of people. But there were phones outside the station too, and might be easier to reach, so hefting my case, I worked against the crowd to the turnstiles, then through a little corridor to arrive at the entrance to the GO bus terminal.

The out-of-town buses were steadily arriving,

disgorging people into the already crammed TTC station. There was a queue to use the phones here as well, but not as bad, and I leaned against the beige-painted cinderblocks to wait.

My cell phone was still snug in my pocket, and I took it out. One bar of battery left. It would be better to call Dylan from a pay phone. Five minutes wasn't too long to wait, and I'd still have the cell in an emergency, in case I got delayed again somewhere without a pay phone. I stashed the Nokia back in my pocket since my purse was now full of eSaleEase-branded pens.

Putting the spare pens there turned out to be a mistake.

When my turn came for the pay phones, I had to dig through my purse for my wallet, spilling items in the process. Muttering a profusion of 'shits' and 'craps' under my breath, I gathered up the pens and makeup while simultaneously trying to search through the outer pocket of my presentation case, aware of the people waiting behind me, the impatience blasting off them in waves comparable to the reflected sunshine off a nearby GO bus windshield.

Finally recognizing the dire depths of the situation, I scrambled to push everything out of the way so that the person tapping their foot behind me could use the phone instead. Crouching in a corner, I dumped everything out of my purse.

My heart thumped against the inside of my ribs, like someone knocking on a door with bad news.

I pulled out everything from the presentation case's pocket. More pens, mints—why did I have a half packet of old man mints? Those couldn't be mine, they must be Steve's from accounting—some pennies, a folded-up brochure. Serviettes.

No wallet.

I patted my jacket down but the only useful pocket had my cell phone. My skirt had no pockets at all but I patted my thighs anyway, because that's what you do when you have lost your wallet outside the farthest station from home when there's a power outage and confused crowds and August heat: you pat down everywhere.

I even opened up the presentation case to search through it, despite knowing I'd had my wallet in my purse since I left Darlington because I'd needed—

Shit.

Shit shit *shit*, my metropass!

This was way worse than not having a quarter for a pay phone. Now I had no credit card, no debit or cash, and *no way to get back into the TTC station.*

I'd fallen down in the bus loop; my wallet must have slipped out of my purse; someone must have accidentally kicked it away from me; I didn't notice I didn't have it because I was in such a rush to get out of the way.

"Fucking fucketty fuck fuck." Taking a deep breath, I smoothed my hair back and wiped my face. That trickle of sweat running down between my shoulder blades had become a torrent and it itched. No one paid me any attention; they had their own problems as the GO buses continued to arrive, and the feet flowed around me like a river around a stone.

My wallet might still be there.

A rough chance but I had to try. I scooped everything into the presentation case—including my useless purse—and straightened up, tugging down my skirt and taking another couple of deep breaths for courage before rejoining the current.

I didn't have a metropass, and I didn't have any money. But I'd already paid the fare boarding the bus, right? Didn't that count for something? I didn't have a transfer, hadn't needed one, I had had my metropass. Smoothing down my blouse and jacket, I decided to just wing it. There was enough commotion near the fare gates that I could probably just slip by, fetch my wallet, and continue home.

They'd closed the fare collectors' booth and opened the wheelchair accessible gates. A large, heavy-set man in maroon TTC livery sat in a chair in the middle of the open gate, checking people's passes with greater speed than the turnstile would have allowed. Good for the station; bad for me. I swallowed and set my shoulders straight and dovetailed into the line, trying to look confident, like I had everything under control.

One of the employees out in the loop produced a megaphone from somewhere, trying to direct people to shuttle buses; his megaphone died in a series of squeals and he gave it a smack, as though corporal punishment improved battery life.

Four ahead of me was an older woman frantically going through her oversized purse, pulling out Kleenexes, knitting, endless receipts and papers. The heavy-set fare collector—who had a severe squint and looked more cross than Catholic school, red-faced in the heat—sighed very heavily and waved her through, barking at her to keep the line moving.

I swung around my presentation case so that it would be between me and the fare collector, and once I was in his view started pawing through the outer pocket I knew to be full of pens and mints. It worked; the fare collector grunted with impatience, already primed.

"Sorry, I know it's in here," I said with face-scrunching apology, scattering pens like bird seed, crouching down to pick them up, being as fumble-fingered as possible—which wasn't that much of an act. "Sorry! Sorry, everything's a mess—"

He cleared his throat in disgust. "Can't you women ever get these things in your hand before I need to see them? Every goddamn day. You're holding up the line, just—" He made a vague gesture.

I twitched a little bit, but then, playing up annoying female stereotypes was my plan in the first place. "Thank you! I'm so sorry, really, thank you—" I swept everything up into my arms and made an exaggerated high-heel scurry through the fare area.

Once I was in the concourse proper I gave a sigh while stuffing everything into my presentation case again, including my purse, before scanning the ground near where I'd fallen.

Clenching and unclenching my fists, presentation case slung around my back like an oversized hippie's guitar, I circled outward, my head down, searching. The sun had shifted, glinting off all the glass and chrome, blindingly bright when least expected. Twice I thought I saw my wallet and hurried over only to discover a candy bar wrapper or a bit of paper bag.

A dull throb pressed behind my eyes. My wallet was gone; someone had probably seen it, picked it up, and— I dashed over to the trio of garbage cans near the escalators. Newspapers, more food wrappers, drinks— there. Red-brown leather: my wallet.

After fishing it out, my triumph morphed to ashes. The wallet was empty. Hollowed out. Whatever cash I'd had left over from lunch; spare change; credit and bank cards.

My metropass.

All gone.

I wiped my hands clean on my jacket and rubbed the bridge of my nose, deliberating. So much for that. Still,

I was inside the fare zone, I could just grab a shuttle bus and deal with replacing everything tomorrow—

Someone grabbed my right arm above the elbow. I jumped about a foot and tried to twist away. It was the squinting fare collector.

"Excuse *me*, miss." His tone was a growl, the *miss* heavily sarcastic; he was close enough to my face that spit hit my cheeks and I recoiled again. "Can I see your pass, *please*?"

I froze. Clearing my throat—my lips suddenly dry—I began: "My wallet was stolen—look—"

"I knew it," Squints snarled, his meaty hand still around my arm. "You thought you could get by without paying your fare!"

"My wallet was stolen," I repeated. Out of my peripheral vision, one of the shuttle buses pulled up only a few paces away. "Please. I will fix it tomorrow—"

"Yeah, yeah. I hear everything you downtown bitches try on me."

I blinked. "...Excuse me?"

"You heard me. I might not catch everyone who gets by me, but I caught *you*, and I'm going to make sure you stay caught." Yanking on my arm, he tried to force me back in the direction of the fare office.

"Let go of me!" I struggled and slapped at his hand, but the presentation case was heavy on my shoulders and in the way. I'd never known one of the fare collectors to get up close and personal like this. "I'll walk there myself."

"Too late for that, lady. You think you're the only one having a rough day? Huh? Always excuses with you people—" He was strong, and he was dragging me. "Head Office says I gotta start making examples, and believe me, lady, you are *it*. You wait until I call them—"

"Yeah?" The throb of my headache was replaced by an angry pulse. Yes, okay, I had jumped the turnstile, but I had technically already paid the fare once, and anyway, I didn't need to be manhandled like this. He was hurting me over a $2 fare. "How are you going to call anyone, huh? Power's out, remember?"

Squints gave me a grimace, like I was some sort of contagious moron, and dug his fingernails in. He put his disgusting jowls too close to mine and I fought an irrational urge to bite his nose. "I got a direct line to Head Office."

"Yeah? Direct line, huh? Good, because I want to talk to them myself." I couldn't pry his fingers off me without getting free of the presentation case, which, as of this moment, held all of my belongings. "I'm going to tell them how I already paid a fare, and you're hurting me."

"Head Office isn't gonna talk to *you*."

I pulled back, yanking my arm away and nearly dislocating my shoulder in the process. Squints didn't like that, his face flushing a deeper red. I was making it harder for him to maintain his grip, and we were attracting attention from other people in the concourse.

Gathered by the stairs was a knot of confused tourists with dangling cameras on straps and oversized backpacks, gesturing among themselves. They obviously hadn't heard or understood the instructions about the shuttle buses, and it gave me an idea. "Here!" I shouted at them, pointing with my free hand at Squints. "He can help you! Ask him! He knows where to go! Come here! *He has free maps!*"

Squints swivelled around, blinking with confusion—as the bewildered travellers bore down on him, holding out their paper transfers, asking endless questions in broken English. Only a few yards away, the shuttle bus's back doors were closing. I wrenched myself free, then took off at a sprint.

"Hey!" Squints shouted after me. Then: "Head Office wants to talk to you!" but yet another regular bus was already disembarking, spewing even more confused commuters into the overcrowded concourse.

I wove around and through them, ignoring the stabbing pains in my heel, arm, and shoulder, before leaping onto the shuttle bus, twisting around to yell, "You tell Head Office to go fuck themselves!" just as the front doors closed.

I leaned on the glass, breathing hard. The driver stared at me, confused. "What the hell? You all right?"

"Yeah," I said smoothly, running a hand down my blouse, trying to breathe normally. "Some crazy person tried to attack me. But I'm okay."

"You sure?"

I nodded, vigorously. The driver craned around me for a second, but then shrugged and gestured for me to move away from the door. There was an empty seat near the front and I lurched towards it as the shuttle bus pulled away from the curb.

I fell into the seat, peering out the window, spotting Squints at the edge of the terminal. I gave a jaunty wave. He responded, rather curiously, by making his hand into a mock phone, ranting into it, purple-faced, while shaking his other fist. I flashed him my middle finger and then leaned back, still breathing hard but starting to relax, the pain in my shoulder ebbing.

At least I had a seat to Kennedy.

3.
DYLAN

You glance at the timer on the oven, forgetting that it's out, its retro hands frozen at 4:13. Part of the reason you leased this apartment was the gas stove. One, the cooking is simply better, but two, it's usable if the power goes out. Maybe not the pilot lighter, but that's okay, there's matches.

The oven, of course, is a different story. Thankfully the roast was well on its way to being done, and if it stays in the well-insulated oven—provided you don't forget and open the door—it should coast the rest of the way. Maybe it'll be still rare in the centre but you can just give Mallory the end pieces. She won't mind. She seems to prefer boot leather to properly cooked.

The potatoes can be boiled on the stove-top instead of roasted, that's fine.

All that's left is the balsamic for the vinaigrette. It should have been easy enough for Mallory to pick up on her way home, the grocery store is en route from the station, but she didn't call back.

You glance at the stove-top clock, blink, and then reflexively check the DVD player. Right. No power there either, not even a blinking 12:00.

Watches. Where's your father's old watch?

It's here buried in your sock drawer. You should probably clean that out one of these days, but on the other hand, you don't care. It takes thirty seconds to root through a drawer. What's the hurry? You find the watch between two balled socks. Golden clunky '70s style garbage that you'd never wear—ever—but it'll do for now.

Papa gave it to you thinking you'd be really pleased—and you were, but there was no way you could explain that it wasn't the watch you liked, it was the memories. Getting to sit on the couch with Papa after he came home from work while dinner finished cooking. You'd play with the watch and its intricate links and listen to him complain about customers or brag about a good sale, one arm around your shoulders, the other with a glass of rum.

Mallory told you a similar story once, about the clock on her grandmother's mantle. She was allowed to wind it when she visited, it was a grown-up responsibility that they trusted to her, and she was only seven, and she remained proud of that for years until she found a similar clock at a garage sale and realized that it was both incredibly easy to wind and also had a hidden battery back-up. You'd both laughed, the dishes cleaned, second round of drinks, she told the story really well, you could practically see her face as she realized she'd been lovingly duped all these years.

Clocks and watches. Time and memories.

You asked if she'd bought the clock as a memento because at the time you didn't know Mal as well, you didn't know that she wasn't particularly sentimental about stuff. For her it was all about the story, the anecdote that she could fashion from it to be carried in the back of her mind, ready for an opportunity; for you it was about holding the object and losing yourself in that singular moment, reliving it.

That and you couldn't bear to tell Papa how ugly the watch is. He was being so thoughtful.

You slip it on and fasten it and it catches arm hair and pulls. God, it's ugly. But it's still ticking. You have no idea if it's correct or not, it might have slowed down. Still, that shouldn't matter for timing potatoes.

It's only when you get back to the kitchen that you remember you have a perfectly good tomato-shaped food timer on top of the refrigerator, coated in dust. Oh well. The detour was worth it.

4.
SCROUNGING FOR CHANGE

Normally in the course of a subway delay or 'unscheduled downtime', there are replacement shuttle buses on the scene. That's what happened at Scarborough Town Centre, right? I confidently expected that by the time we reached Kennedy either the subway would be running again or the shuttle bus situation would be sorted out. There might be a lot of people, sure, but they'd have staff organizing and directing the crowd.

Instead it was pandemonium.

I slipped off the shuttle bus, wary. Even in the bus loop people were already pushing and shoving.

"Sorry, folks," the driver shouted from behind me at the people trying to push their way on while we disembarked. "I gotta go out of service. Gotta fuel up. Can't reach anyone on the radio at the station."

"There's no gas stations," someone else shouted.

No gas stations?

"Whole city's down," someone else remarked confidently. "Just got off the phone with someone in Markham. They don't have power either."

"I just called my brother in Newmarket. They're down too."

Newmarket? Markham? Was the whole greater Toronto area without power? How does that even happen?

The bus driver shooed me away from the door and I used my presentation case to push space for myself, the gathered crowd reluctantly backing away. But dimly, through the commotion, I realized what those two statements had in common: nearby pay phones. I could call Dylan!

Fuck. I had no money. Not having any money on me was such a weird concept that I kept bumping into it, like an end table in a hallway. This was the first time I'd had my wallet stolen; I'd misplaced it at home before but never in a public place where its contents could get pilfered. I had no money and I still had to get home.

I supposed I could bum a quarter off someone, but I really didn't want to do that. It made me feel unclean, the idea of asking a complete stranger for money. And things weren't that bad yet. Dylan probably wasn't even worried. Maybe annoyed that I hadn't called him back when I said I would, but it was probably fine.

If the city's grid really was down, I'd have to take shuttle buses the entire length, and that would take hours. Longer if I had to get off at transfer points and then re-board. And I didn't have a paper transfer so I'd have to be careful to stay in fare-paid zones. Where to next? The station was a chaotic stew of people pushing, shouting, milling about aimlessly, and/or waving their arms at other people. Some people make like Kermit the Frog at the smallest thing; I don't get it. But whatever.

Focus, Mallory!

Fuck, I was sweaty. Sweaty and hungry.

Focus!

Even in heels, it was hard to see past people's heads, shoulders, and gesticulating arms, so I found a convenient lamp post in a concrete holder and hauled myself up on it to scan the area. Buses kept arriving but few left, and that was causing the build-up. But across the bus loop was a bank of pay phones.

I scrabbled back down, secured my presentation case, and began my swim upstream.

The beating sun overhead and stress of the compressed crowd meant that B.O. hung in the still, humid air, almost a taste more than a smell. Sweat ran down my back like Niagara Falls. I felt disgusting and rapidly running out of my last nerves, but my goal was small: find a quarter; call Dylan before his handset's battery ran out; reassure him that I would be home as soon as I could. Then worry about how I would do that.

As a teenager living in a small town, I had had ample time on my hands, and one skill I'd developed from the time period was identifying and scanning key patches of ground where people might drop money and not notice. Since becoming an adult with a full-time job, I was less in need of spare change and so less mindful myself of picking up coins I'd dropped. Circle of life, I suppose. Like a deer carcass fertilizing the woodland soil or something.

I paced around the phones, circling around by the entrance closest to the Kiss'n'Ride, eyes glued to cracks in the asphalt, ignoring anything coppery. People in a hurry, you see; that's the key. Particularly men. Men because they are likely to keep their change loose in their front pockets. Then, when they run for their morning train, they jam their hands in the pockets for their metropass or their wallet, and coins are spilled in the rush. Bills too, sometimes.

(Since women are more likely to keep things in a purse due to lack of pockets in their garments, they are less likely to spill change without noticing. I myself often have quite the collection of change in my big purse, which of course I wasn't wearing today. If I had been, I wouldn't be in this fucking situation, hunting lost quarters like a teenager outside an arcade.)

I felt ridiculous—and tired, and angry—but my options were: hunt for coins or mill around aimlessly waiting for a shuttle bus that might not exist. At least on the periphery of the crowd it was marginally cooler and much less smelly.

There.

A glint of silver. I crouched down and picked out the dime with my fingernails. A whole quarter would have been better but it was a start. There—another dime. Not far off now.

Across the street was the Kiss'n'Ride, the area where people dropped commuters off in the morning or picked them up in the evening. To my left, past the peeling-painted metal barrier, lay a wide, spacious parking lot, like a field growing glinting windshields. Definitely quarters out there—maybe even a loonie. But if I left the fare-paid area, I'd have the same problem getting back in that I did at Scarborough Town Centre. That squinty red-faced ogre had been really scary, and I didn't feel like tempting luck twice.

After a few more sweaty minutes of scanning the ground, I admitted defeat. I had two dimes. Still a nickel short. I sat down on the curb to figure out my next move.

A group marched across the bus terminal, scattering people in their wake like dogs and seagulls. All dressed alike in expensive black business wear: suits on the men; high-heels and skirt-suits on the women, with unflattering buns and carefully applied makeup even in the sweaty mess of the afternoon. Leather briefcases.

Lawyers.

One of them, an older white guy with the shaved head of the recently balding, shook his cell phone in outrage. I couldn't hear him but his body language and reddening face spoke to indignation. Probably at being delayed by more than thirty seconds; the faces of his colleagues were carefully composed masks. I imagine he was the sort of guy who blew his top over every minor inconvenience, having worked with various Joe Volcanoes in many different offices and careers over the years. One didn't have to do very much to get caught in their crossfire—especially if one was junior and female—so believe me when I tell you I felt no sympathy, none at all, as I watched him pull something out of his jacket pocket while not paying attention and let a crisp green twenty flutter to the pavement.

No one else noticed. None of them paid him any attention; one of the women actually stepped on the bill, momentarily spearing it under her heels, causing my breath to catch in my throat.

No, no, no no no nononono...

...and she was through the fence.

Goddammit.

I looked back at the phones, then made up my mind.

I grabbed my presentation case, heaved it over the barrier, and slid through. The lawyers were all getting into a car, Joe Volcano still spluttering on about something. They drove away—cutting someone else off as they did so—and I hurried over. The bill just lay there. I swooped down and picked it up before it could flutter away.

Yes, I was outside the paid zone, yes, I didn't have a metropass, but now I had a solid twenty. Maybe you're thinking that I'd go and break it somewhere for change for a phone—but you'd be wrong. You'd be focusing on the small plan when the bigger opportunity beckons.

I tucked the twenty in my bra strap—I no longer trusted my pockets, and no longer cared about germs; I was rank and tired enough that whatever cocaine was on that lawyer's money could only improve matters. Straightening up, tightening my ponytail, and thanking the heavens for people with more money than sense, I trotted through the parking lot with my presentation case slung over my shoulder toward the Kiss'n'Ride and the waiting taxis.

I waved at the closest one, but before I could cross the street, I got sniped by a businessman in a dark blue pinstriped suit, dashing out from the shaded overhang and into the back seat.

Weird. I hadn't seen him. But then I hadn't been looking at the interior of the Kiss'n'Ride. I'd missed the light, so I stood waiting. In the time it took for the light to change, yes, another person streaked out ahead of me and took the next cab before I could get there. Fine. There would be more soon.

Making a snap decision, I abandoned the Kiss'n'Ride area and moved closer to Eglinton Avenue. Traffic flowed smoothly, growing my optimism. Not long to find a free cab now—lots passed by but with their lights off, already bearing passengers.

But as I waited on the side of the street, that initial optimism began to ebb. Maybe I should go back to the station entrance, see if anyone else was going to Etobicoke, then band together to order a cab and split the fare. I had scrap paper in my presentation case and pens—so many pens—so I could figure something out.

Probably. Probably more doable than the crazy idea I had in my head anyway.

Ready to admit defeat and walk back to the station, I lifted up my case and saw yellow out of the corner of my eye. A cab! He was in the east-bound lane, and traffic was stopped. I waved at him, and he saw me, and waved back through the open window. But there was nowhere he could go.

Hairs prickled at the back of my neck. I checked over my shoulder and yes—someone was swaggering towards the busy street: another businessman. What was the deal with these guys anyway? Didn't they understand the time-honoured code of 'finders keepers' and 'I called it'?

What was I saying—of course they didn't. These guys thought they came first in everything. Well, not today, buddy.

I checked both ways (partly habit and partly because I am a sensible adult) and then I launched myself out into Eglinton (a sensible adult who sometimes launches herself into traffic). Business Guy moved to intercept. We'd both scented the taxi (bad metaphor, I admit) and were on the hunt. But I wasn't going to let him beat me this time.

Sidling between momentarily idling cars with my presentation case, splitting my attention between the business guy behind me and the traffic in case it started moving—I waved at the cab driver to pop the trunk so I could deposit the bulky case, and then breathlessly slid into the back seat just as traffic resumed, the blockage cleared.

"Are you crazy?" the taxi driver asked me, bemused.

"A little bit. How about you?" I tugged down my skirt as it had ridden up while scooting over the back seat, and peered out the back window. Business Guy had vanished. I relaxed. "Been a day. Did you hear that the power's down all over the city?"

"I did," the driver admitted. The traffic light flashed green and he returned his attention to the wheel. "The roads are insane. No one knows how to drive. Stop and go all the way from Pickering, at least. Where are we going today?"

"As far as twenty dollars will get me," I replied, pulling it out of my bra. His eyebrows leapt out of frame in the rear-view mirror. A young guy, perhaps new on the job. Certainly didn't match the picture of the guy on the license hanging over the back seat (twenty years older and about fifty pounds heavier).

"What does that mean?"

"It means my wallet got stolen, I have no phone, this is all the money I have in the world."

The driver's eyes flicked back between the road and mine. "How far do you think that'll take you?"

"In a perfect world, Etobicoke."

He gave a bark of a laugh. "It's far from a perfect world, miss."

Didn't I know it. So I flashed my watch. "Twenty bucks and a nice watch you can give as a gift to someone."

He smirked. "That's not a valuable watch."

"No, no it's not. But it's not a *junky* watch either, and it's new. I bought it last week. It's at least worth another fifty. Saves you having to buy your girlfriend or niece or mom or someone a birthday present." I mentally crossed my fingers.

He wasn't convinced.

I sighed. "Okay. Plan B. I have some money at home. Grocery cash. Not that much, but it'll cover the rest of the fare. Take the twenty and the watch as a deposit, and I'll pay you the rest when I get home. How does that sound? Or you can let me off at the next corner; up to you. But you'd be doing me a huge favour, and that's the sort of good deed that pays forward." Good deed my ass; he was going to make the fare plus get a watch into the bargain. But it was a watch I'd bought on impulse and didn't particularly like, so I didn't care.

The driver deliberated, but then flicked the 'occupied' sign onto his meter, and held his hand behind the seat. I gave him both the found twenty and the watch and settled in as he turned south on Midland.

The taxi stank of hot leatherette and old cigarettes, even with the windows open. But it was a seat, a moving seat, heading west along Danforth. The traffic was stop-and-go, clogged with more than the usual rush-hour traffic since the subway was down, and with the traffic lights out, there were more than a few accidents amid the confusion.

But none of that was my problem any more.

"Do you think it's as far as Mississauga?" the driver asked. "The power out?"

"No idea. Someone at the station said Markham. And Newmarket."

He drummed his fingers on the wheel. "That's pretty far."

"If it's that far north, then maybe... the whole grid's down."

"What? Everywhere?" He panicked for a second and then relaxed into a plainer, simpler bewilderment. "That can't be true."

I tried to remember what I'd gleaned from our team research into the Darlington power plant. "Probably all of southern Ontario. I think eastern Ontario is on a different grid. I'm not sure."

He grumbled to himself. "At least it's summer time and not winter. People would die in the winter."

"True." It made me recall the big ice storm when I was a kid. We'd had three days without power but my aunt and uncle had a wood-burning stove in their rec room so we'd bundled into the car and stayed with them and we all played board games while wrapped up in blankets. It had been kinda fun, in a break-from-routine sort of way. Like a second Christmas in January. But I'd been a kid, so I hadn't had to worry about food spoiling or carbon monoxide poisoning or anything like that, just whether or not my brothers or boy cousins were cheating at Monopoly (which they were. A fight broke out and we'd all been sentenced to put on snowsuits and play in the backyard as punishment).

I realized the driver was asking me something. "Sorry?"

He wasn't speaking to me but to the dispatcher. Either the dispatcher had power in their neighbourhood, or a generator or batteries or something like that. I wondered which and tried not to look like I was eavesdropping.

But the driver was watching me in the rear-view mirror, and switched from English to a different language. His voice dropped into a low whisper and his body language grew tight and withdrawn.

My neck hairs prickled again.

He pulled over by the side of the street. "What's up?" I asked, keeping my voice light.

"You need to get out here," he said, very tense and no longer making eye contact. "I can't get caught up in that kind of trouble. I'm very sorry."

"Trouble? What trouble? Look, I know this isn't a usual kind of payment, but—"

He'd got out, the engine still running, the door wide.

He flung open the back door and gestured for me to get out. "What's the matter? I thought—hey!" When I hadn't moved, he'd reached in to grab me.

"We can't be caught up in that," he kept repeating. "I don't want any trouble."

"I don't want any trouble either! Let go of me!" But I didn't brace myself in time and between his yank on my arm and the slitheriness of the leatherette, I slid half out and had to catch myself. "Okay! Okay, jeez. Careful. Let me go. Let's figure this out."

"Nothing to figure out," he said, quickly and firmly. "I don't want to be caught up in any Head Office trouble. I'm very sorry."

"You said that," I muttered, climbing to my feet, brushing myself off. "But we can—" With rising horror I realized he was already back in his seat. I grabbed the door handle, but he'd locked them from the inside. "Hey! Stop! *Hey!*" He pulled into traffic. "Hey! You took my money! And my watch!" and then the full realization smacked me and I ran after him, waving both arms like a lunatic. "You've got my case! *You still have my case in your trunk!*"

Another car honked behind me and I scrambled back onto the sidewalk.

Fuck.

5.
DYLAN

It's after six. Where the hell is Mallory? She said she was going to call from the station; that was two hours ago!

The heat in the apartment is stifling, so you grab a beer from the fridge and head out onto the deck. The outside air isn't much better, it's like a wet towel, but perhaps not a *hot* wet towel and you'll take what you can get. Someone told you that Toronto was built on swampland, and every July and August, you believe it.

The beer's still cold, that's a good sign, and plenty refreshing. The patio is small, just enough for a little picnic table that's probably older than you are, carved with the initials of so many previous tenants and guests that it's more carving than wood, but still holds together. Well, that one leg is flaking but it's cosmetic. You rest the beer against the wooden railing, looking at what's visible in the slivers between the surrounding buildings. At the right angle and on a super clear day you can see Lake Ontario. Mallory thinks it's not the lake but the top of the parking garage; it's too faint to tell. It's silvery grey and flat and south, so it could well be the lake.

Smells waft up from one of the apartments. Or, no, someone is in the parking lot behind the health-food store, they've wheeled out an ancient barbeque from somewhere and they're grilling. Smells like beef with a miso-marinade. Mouth-watering.

The power's been out long enough on the block that people are getting inventive for dinner; maybe it's time you did the same. You could get some miso yourself and make a dressing. Cold sliced roast, potato salad, the chives are growing nicely, they'll be a good addition, sprinkle them over everything. The mayo should still be good, after all, the beer was cold, it takes a while for a fridge to change temperature if you keep the door closed; like the oven, but, you know, cold.

There's a knock at the door. Startled, you straighten, hopeful that it's Mallory. Maybe she forgot her keys again. She was in a rush this morning what with that presentation case and having to be downtown early to catch a ride with her boss. She refused to be sensible and take a larger purse. Something about the line of her outfit.

The knock comes again, but it sounds familiar, and not like Mallory's.

You pad across the apartment, still holding the beer, and open it. It's Camila from across the hall. "Hi."

She smiles at you. "Your power out too?" You can see her gaze drift over your shoulder into the apartment, searching for signs of electricity.

"I think it's the whole block," you answer in English, taking a sip of beer.

"I heard on my little radio," she continues in Spanish, "that it's the whole city. Maybe even further. Maybe down into New York."

"The state or the city?"

She cocks her head, confused, and then laughs. "Oh. I don't know, they didn't say."

You wonder how a whole city would cope without power. Especially a giant city like New York.

She's leaning against the door jamb, watching you under her eyelashes. On the one hand, you have a patio and she does not and her ancient living-room window-rattler won't be working. On the other hand, you can imagine Mallory won't be pleased to come home after a long day and find you entertaining your neighbour—whom she distrusts for some reason—on the patio, just the two of you.

Camila's still waiting. From outside you can smell the steaks cooking. It's well after when Mallory should be home. She might be stuck on a shuttle bus somewhere, inching across town.

Fuck it.

"Come on and sit outside where it's cool," you say, pushing the door open. "Bring your radio and tell the neighbours. We'll turn this into a party."

6.
DOIN' IT OLD SCHOOL

I wasn't sure how long I'd been walking. I mean, I could probably count in blocks (if I really wanted to, which I did not), but now that the taxi guy had my watch, I couldn't check the time. I suppose I could have turned on my phone, which was all that I had left, but didn't want to accidentally drain its perplexing battery. Better to save it for an emergency.

Trudging along this stretch of Danforth was depressing. It was like a never-ending strip mall, all small bargain stores with names like 'Best Prices!' and a stack of brooms outside. All of them seemed to have brooms stacked outside. Either Scarberians went through a lot of brooms or there was a factory near by. Discount brooms. Outlet brooms.

God, my feet hurt.

But at this point I was resigned to walking and I wasn't the only one. Mostly people flowed in the opposite direction than me, and then up side streets. Everyone wore the same staggered 'I can't believe it's this hot and I'm walking home' face, many in outfits chosen for an air-conditioned office, blazers slung over their arms. Apart from my westbound direction, I fit in.

I'd taken off my jacket around Victoria Park. That was a while ago, so I guess it wasn't fair to make fun of Scarborough for its broom obsession when the mockery should be squarely directed at East York. Yorkians? Yorkies, I decided, like the small dogs. East Yorkies and North Yorkies.

Food smells were torments wafting from open doorways. A lot of restaurants had set up tables outside to sell at a discount; either that or throw the food away, I supposed. Didn't matter to me, since all I had to my name was a company phone and two dimes I'd found in a filthy parking lot. All the same, I kept glancing at the ground for that last, elusive nickel.

Dylan probably knew by now that I wasn't going to be home for dinner. Our little stretch of Islington Village is pretty neighbourly; news of the extent of the blackout had no doubt been passed around, patio to patio. Knowing I had a meeting out at Darlington today, he'd put two and two together and eat dinner on his own.

My nose wrinkled. No doubt Camila was knocking on his door, fluttering her very long eyelashes and seeing if she could borrow a cup of electricity.

Or maybe they were all having a patio party, eating my special dinner. *My* special dinner, made with love, for *me*.

I was, by this point, starting to feel a little sorry for myself. The food smells weren't helping.

Ahead of me on the Danforth, two cars smashed into each other with a squeal of brakes and crash-tinkle of broken glass. Someone shrieked from the surprise. Both drivers leapt out of their respective vehicles, examining damage and yelling at each other; neither had stopped at the intersection.

Gradually, once people on the sidewalks realized no one was hurt, they stopped rubbernecking and resumed trudging. I imagine the same scene was being repeated all over the city.

A small restaurant owner came out, reporting to 911 on a handset tucked between his chin and shoulder while wiping his hands on his apron. Shouting out questions to the two drivers, who abandoned their cars there on the Danforth, continuing to berate each other while the cook acted as a go-between. And yet, within moments, he offered to give them each something to eat and to let them sit while they waited. The two shook hands, and disappeared into the restaurant.

That made me feel a little better.

Traffic jammed up against the accident. I kept walking, trying not to peer at the scene; it was just a simple fender-bender, no one was hurt, police would be along eventually. Maybe the cook/owner would call a tow-truck. Nothing to see here, move along, move along...

But then something else caught my eye, and I stopped.

A small beige Hyundai was stalled directly behind the accident, too close to the broken cars to go around without scraping them and no one behind them was willing to give them space to back up or turn into the other lane. But that's not what caught my eye; it was the piece of paper in the back seat window that said 'Humber' in ballpoint pen.

I strolled up. "Hi," I said, through the open passenger window. "You kids Humber students?"

Four young, fresh, possibly stoned faces peered back up at me. The driver was the least bleary-eyed, looking instead startled and alarmed, no doubt from seeing the accident happen in front of them.

"Yeah," said the front-seat passenger, who looked me up and down, and then squinted. "We're giving lifts to other students? The subway's down, you know. There's, like, a big power out."

You don't say. "I'm going in that direction," I told them. "But I don't have any money for gas. Wallet was stolen."

"That's terrible," said someone from the back seat. He prodded the driver. "We totally have a seat here in the middle, right Josh?"

The girl in the front seat seemed unconvinced. I held my arms out, in submission. "I'm not an axe murderer."

"That's what an axe murderer would say," the driver, Josh, muttered, but he was distracted, trying to figure out what to do. I held out a finger, the international signal for *uno momento, s'il vous plait,* and walked carefully in front of them, dodging the broken glass and noting the hissing sound from one of the cars. Cars don't explode like they do in the movies, right? I slipped my jacket back on to keep my hands free.

Traffic was slow enough from rubber-necking that even if something did hit me it would barely leave a bruise. So it was easy to march out into traffic like I owned it, and hold up my hands in either direction for the east-bound lane to stop. Which they did. Possibly out of surprise, but I like to think it was my air of confidence.

Directing Josh into the newly calmed east-bound lane, he managed to creep around the accident, before immediately pulling over. I directed traffic to continue, and now with enough space and warning to dodge the accident, the drivers understood the need to take turns and divert into the other lane. I scurried to the safety of the curb and the open door.

"Thanks, lady," Josh said. "You're... a student?"

"No," I admitted, squeezing into an incredibly crowded back seat. There were two college kids there already, each with backpacks on their laps. The footwells had stuff in them, the rear windshield was almost entirely blocked, and the smell of skunk, cheap patchouli, and compressed humanity made my eyes water a bit. "But I live near there." That was not true and I amended it. "I live in that direction, anyway."

"That's cool," Josh confirmed, watching the traffic like a kingfisher. "We're all starting there next week."

"Moving in," my fellow backseater said, brightly, blond dreads shaking with the froshiest of excitement. "We're going to be roommates. Except Laurel."

"I have a different house," Laurel in the front seat explained.

"That's great," I replied when it became clear that they were waiting for my blessing. "Sounds like you'll all have a great time, college is so much fun!" Those were magic words and the car's occupants accepted me as one of their own, Blond Dreads even pulling out a joint and offering me first drag.

"Lincoln! I told you, not in the car, man!" Josh hesitantly rejoined traffic.

"Josh's first time driving in the city," Laurel told me, girl-to-girl.

I was so squeezed I could barely breathe. "What a day for it."

"I know, right?"

"C'mon," Josh chided.

There was silence for a couple of blocks, punctuated by soft snoring: the girl on the other side of Lincoln fell asleep, her face pressed against the sheet of paper that said HUMBER on it.

"So where are you kids from then?" I asked super brightly, feeling approximately 150 years old, but glad to be sitting down and moving not under my own power.

"Oshawa," Lincoln answered. "Except Laurel."

"Whitby," Laurel supplied.

"Oh. That's nice." I had no opinions on anything east of Morningside. Morningside was only included in my opinions because I had fond memories of the Metro Zoo. "Nice area." I mean, I assumed.

"So boring," Laurel replied. "But we're in the big city now! It's going to be great!" Much whooping at this, waking up the snorer, who blearily peered around, decided we weren't there yet, and went back to sleep, this time against the backpack on her lap. Laurel had the tone of someone who was desperately trying to convince herself that she was having a great time. I could sympathize.

Josh, meanwhile, was indeed nervous driving along the Danforth, especially since there seemed to be a great many people who weren't being as cautious. He turned to Laurel, whispering: "How much further?"

"To Humber? Quite a while I'm afraid," I replied, leaning forward.

He looked startled. "No, to her uncle's?"

I blinked. "...uncle's?"

"We're stopping at my aunt and uncle's," Laurel explained. "They have, like, a box of dishware or something for the house? Like, a housewarming present?"

I took a deep breath. It was probably fine. I was sitting and we were moving. "...and where are they?"

Laurel consulted a piece of paper. "Uh. St. Clair and Avenue."

Heavenly ones, save me from the stupid, ignorant, and stoned. "Oh." Carefully, I paused, as if considering, and then asked: "And what route are you taking?"

"Uh, Danforth to Bloor," Josh began, with the tone of someone reciting. "Then right on Avenue—"

"I'm going to stop you right there." I took a deep breath for patience. "How about we figure out a faster route with less traffic than the busiest non-highway in the city?"

We turned north on Coxwell, then left on O'Connor, which flowed significantly faster. The traffic lights were still out, but away from the Danforth it seemed like more people were driving carefully, treating all intersections as four-way-stops and so on. There were bits of glass on the road here too, but much less commotion in general, and Josh grew confident, especially since the area around O'Connor looked more, well, suburban, and I imagine that brought comforting memories of Oshawa. I gave them directions through Donlands and over the valley towards Mount Pleasant; a longer trip maybe in kilometers but smoother and easier for all concerned.

I leaned back, relaxing, although a headache crept around the side of my head, spreading like damp across a basement wall. Lincoln noticed me rubbing my temple and offered me another drag. I replied no with a wan smile and cracked the window.

"Man, I told you," Josh barked over his shoulder. "Not in the car!"

Once we passed through Mt. Pleasant, the area turned from suburban detached homes to apartment buildings and offices, and Josh resumed driving like he was in a demilitarized zone with an enemy flag waving.

I leaned forward. "Hey, Laurel?"

"Yeah?"

"Do you think your aunt would let me use the

phone?"

"Oh, for sure. She's, like, really nice. I'm sure that's fine."

"You're not going to be long, right?" Josh asked, but whether to me or his seatmate was unclear, so we both answered in the negative.

"I'm just picking up house stuff, I told you," Laurel added, peeved.

"It's just that it's, like, after six and we're still not there," Josh continued, hunched over the steering wheel, eyeing the road with suspicion. "I don't want to be driving in the city. In the, you know."

"The dark?" Laurel supplied, snidely. "Don't be such a baby. If you're scared to drive, I can drive."

"No you can't, your license got revoked, remember?"

"Oh yeah."

Lincoln nudged me. "Do you drive?"

I do, but I wasn't about to commit to driving a brace of students to an unfamiliar neighbourhood during a blackout in the dark.

"She's not on my insurance, man." Josh's teeth enjoyed audible grinding. "Shut up and let me drive!"

I rested my arm on the open window and enjoyed the breeze, which, while smelling of traffic and hot asphalt, was still better than the inside of the car. I wondered how Dylan was doing. Probably out on the patio. Probably had his feet up and a beer, the lucky bastard. Mind you, it was his day off. Still. All I wanted myself was to be on a patio with a beer, but first I had to get to St Clair and Avenue.

In front of a row of townhouses Laurel burst into action, shouting "here!!" almost at random, punctuated by waving arms and slaps on his shoulder, causing Josh to slam on the brakes, in turn shuddering the packed Hyundai to a halt and slamming us all forward—well, if we had space to slam, anyway. The back seat was so packed that all the momentum did was wake up Juliette, who murmured, "We here yet?" blearily to Lincoln.

Josh parked, and we all tumbled out of the car. I stretched, putting my shoes back on. Even with the detour it shouldn't haven't been that long, but with the cautious driving and constant 4-way stops it became long enough and felt longer. Lincoln stretched too and I caught him eyeing where the back of my shirt had ridden up. I pulled it down and frowned at him but he didn't seem to notice, losing focus and yawning until he remembered something in his backpack and started ferreting around, pulling out a half-eaten granola bar with triumph.

Ugh. I wasn't even hungry anymore. The heat and the stress and the lurchy driving had driven all thoughts of food from me.

Laurel, meanwhile, was on the stoop of one of the plaster gingerbreaded townhouses ringing the doorbell, waiting, and growing ever more confused. "No power!" Josh shouted to her and she startled, before commencing pounding on the door instead.

The tastefully painted front door opened swiftly and a thin, sour-faced woman opened the door. You know the type: overly bleached blonde to cover the greys, matching twinset, heels on even in the house. Face like she'd bitten a Tylenol. I couldn't see her neckline but I imagined she was wearing pearls.

Laurel disappeared into the house, pushing her way past her aunt who regarded us and the overpacked Hyundai with a scowl bordering on disgust. If I hadn't seen what she was looking at I would assume a smear of roadkill or a backed-up toilet.

I smoothed down my skirt and tucked in my white blouse. I probably looked like death, but at least I didn't look like a student. I knew the type of people who owned houses like these; supplication must be made. I started to walk up to the door, fixing a friendly-but-woe-betrodden smile on my face, when Laurel bustled out, carrying a cardboard box with an ancient slow-cooker poking out the top, bedecked in orange and brown—no doubt a wedding present her aunt had never used because cooking was for poor people.

And right behind Laurel was her uncle.

A weird sense of *déjà vu* trickled along my arms and down my legs.

He could have been anyone, should have been anyone. But he was an older white guy, balding with a shaved head and a dark, expensive, blue-green pin-stripe suit. Those guys are everywhere. Right?

His eyes narrowed.

The guy at Kennedy hadn't looked at me, but this guy did. "Laurel Elizabeth," he said slowly, without shifting his gaze. His niece stopped, rolling her eyes and sighing dramatically.

"What?" she demanded. "What did I do now?"

He stepped out onto the stoop, pulling the door shut behind him, and I knew I wasn't going to be allowed to use the phone. "What did your father tell you about picking up hitchhikers?"

Josh looked at me askance. I shrugged, just as surprised.

Laurel tensed. "This isn't the same."

"Do you even know these people?" He crossed his arms.

"I know Josh and Lincoln, obviously!"

"And the other two?"

I blinked. It hadn't occurred to me to ask about the other passenger, assuming she was another housemate. Juliette remained in the car; once she'd ascertained that we were not at Humber she'd gone right back to sleep. Champion.

"God!" Laurel stamped her foot. "You're just as bad as Dad! I know what I'm doing, okay?" Shoving the box of ancient cookware into Josh's arms, she conveyed her displeasure to her aunt and uncle via crossed arms and glaring and other teenage huffery. "There's a blackout, okay? People are *stranded*, you get that? I'm being, like, a *good person*, I'm *helping people out*."

This didn't seem like a family that helped people out on the regular, unless Aunt had a charity she donated to for tax-sheltering purposes. Both of them stared at me like I was coated in the blood of stupid frosh and still holding the knife.

I held my hands out. "I'm sorry if I got—"

"You stop." Laurel spun on her heel to command me. "This isn't about you. This is about them—" thrust finger behind her, "and my dad trying to control my every move, okay?"

Hands still out, I took a step backwards, bumping into Josh while he tried to cram the cardboard box into the space where I'd been sitting. "I'm really sorry about this," he said, without looking at me. "I had a feeling this might happen."

"It's not your fault," I replied. "At least you got me this far."

He straightened up, resting on the door frame. "Humber's still pretty far."

"Yeah."

Laurel and her uncle were now toe-to-toe yelling about 'responsibility' and 'recklessness' and other rwords while the aunt made shushing motions, her eyes darting around to take in the windows where neighbours theoretically watched via binoculars.

"If I leave peacefully, you think they'll shut up and let you guys go?"

He shrugged.

"You know," Lincoln interjected, "this is exactly the sort of reason I don't talk to my family anymore." He dug the joint out of his pocket and the aunt let out a shriek, her hands flying to her mouth, which he ignored, concentrating instead on retrieving a lighter from his cargo-pants pocket. "You know?"

"Man, I told you—"

"Hey, man, I'm not *in* the car, okay? I'm outside, or whatever."

Aunt pantomimed an aneurysm with theatrical gasps, hands fluttering, skin a whiter shade of pale. Laurel remained defiant, and Uncle still stared at me like I'd been responsible for 9/11.

"Thanks for the ride," I told Josh, wearily.

"Yeah, you're welcome," Lincoln replied, magnanimously, offering me one last puff. And you know what? I took it. Just a small hit, but I made sure to blow the smoke out towards Aunt and Uncle, making sure they saw me. Uncle reddened to coronary shades.

"Well, that's it for me; fellas, Laurel, sleeping person who can't hear me." I tossed off a salute at the loaded car. "Have fun at college, study hard, remember not to talk to strangers, blah blah blah, and good luck in traffic." I slung my jacket over my shoulder and started walking.

7.
GIVE PEAS A CHANCE

I limped south down Spadina after cutting diagonally along side streets from St. Clair and Avenue. There had been a nice park full of people, kids, dogs. People playing Frisbee like they were at the beach. Along Spadina itself there were lots of young people hanging about—students, probably; I am pretty sure UoT has housing around here—relaxing on front steps, some with fans, some with portable radios.

It had a gentle, almost retro vibe, like watching TVO footage from the 60s or 70s, except they had power in the 60s and 70s, I guess. Just not cable or internet. Some industrious soul had set up an honest-to-god lemonade stand out of some cardboard boxes. A (sealed) bag of peas floated in the jug, but condensation ran down the sides of the glass and my throat scratched just looking at it.

"A toonie?! For *lemonade*?!" Someone wasn't having it. "It's not even *real* lemonade, it's from a *can*! And there's *peas* in it!"

I closed my eyes and kept walking until out of earshot (and smell) of the arguing lemonade entrepreneur and customer. I wasn't in a hurry. Maybe by the time I got to Spadina Station the power would be back and the subway running, but it was a small hope.

I had long grown convinced I would have to walk all the way back to Etobicoke. But how long had the power outage lasted already? A couple of hours? It wouldn't be that much longer, surely—

—almost like a mirage, I saw a knot of people drinking at the corner. Drinking bottled water, the plastic bottles sparkling in the light.

My pace and pulse quickened a little. Even without my presentation case, I remained slow in my heels, but I was adept at the precarious tip-toed running that such shoes demanded. On the corner there was indeed a guy giving away bottled water. *Giving* it away. "Oh thank you thank you thank you—!"

But then, as if in slow-motion, someone stepped in front of the generous soul, blocking my view. A tall man, shaved-but-balding head almost glinting in the golden early-evening light. Dark blue pinstripe suit. I stopped, uneasy. He slowly turned and willfully made prolonged eye-contact while he drank the last bottle of water, crumpling up the plastic bottle one-handed before pointing at me and tossing it over his shoulder. A heavy-breathed "what the fuuuuck—" wrenched out of my parched lips. He hopped, a little incongruously, onto a push-scooter and slid away into traffic while giving me the finger.

"FUCK YOU, YOU ASSHOLE!" I yelled after him from the middle of the lane before scrambling out of the way of traffic.

The guy with the now-empty cardboard box of water stared at me. "You know him?"

"No," I retorted, smoothing my skirt down, noticing a

long ladder in my tights. "Fuck me." I noticed he was staring at me in that wary 'is she dangerous' sort of way, and I tried to smile and look friendly. "Sorry. It's been a rough day."

"Yeah, I've been hearing that." His look turned to concern and a touch of pity. "You... been out in the sun a while?"

Oh shit. I touched my face gingerly and stinging pain blossomed in return. Sunburn. "I didn't think I'd be walking for this long," I explained. Near us was the verge of a house, a strip of grass no more than a couple of feet wide before bushes and a tall, imposing Victorian apartment building. But it was shade. I sat down and took off my shoes. I had long ladders on both legs and blisters on my baby toes. "My purse got stolen. No metropass, no money." I declined to mention the Nokia in my pocket. It was my secret and I wanted to keep it safe.

"Shit," the man agreed, still holding the cardboard box by a handle. "Where you trying to get home to?"

"Etobicoke. Islington Village." I perked up, hoping, for just a moment, that he was offering a ride. But he wasn't, just sympathy.

"Jeez, that's far. I live just around the corner. The refrigerators in my shop have been off for too long, so I'm emptying them out."

That made me laugh.

"What?" he asked, curious.

"I didn't know bottled water went off," I explained, feeling like an asshole. Here he was being a nice person and I laughed at him.

But he took it in good humour and joined me in the shade. "Nah. I gave away the ice cream and Popsicles first, mostly to regulars coming in, but then I noticed how many people were just walking. Trying to get home. So anything that I'd have to throw out anyway I gave away."

"Still doesn't explain the water."

He shrugged, studying his feet but he was blushing just a smidge.

I grinned and lay back on my hands, enjoying resting and stretching my toes. All around were the sounds of a normal summer day, except perhaps the buzz of air-conditioners. Cicadas whined, friends joked, asphalt crunched under wheels and sneaker leather. Down the street two drivers honked at each other, unaware of the 'treat it like a 4-way stop' guideline. Overhead, wispy white clouds pulled apart like cotton candy, the sky a deep and shimmering blue. "It's actually a gorgeous day."

"It is, yeah." He cocked his head at me, wanting to ask something. Instead he shook his head and got to his feet. "I should go back, keep my dad company. Sorry about the water."

"Not your fault I was too slow," I agreed. Then: "Any Popsicles left?"

"No, sorry."

"Damn."

He waved at me as he headed on towards his store and I waved back. My toes hurt and I had no wallet or purse and my tights were ruined and I was arguably a tomato-head but at least there were some nice people still in the world.

Which only made me think of that asshole business man. Which in turn made me recall the water being given away. Which then made my throat ache from thirst and my skin itch. Lousy nervous system. I stretched. The nice shopkeeper had wandered west; he probably had a corner store somewhere between here and Bathurst. *Maybe if I find it he'll take pity on me and give me a free can of pop.* Required extra walking and no guarantee of anything, but at least the neighbourhood north of Bloor was full of leafy trees to walk under and little parks to rest in—

I sat back up. Parks. The park at Christie Pits! Christie Pits has a pool! It'll have working water fountains—

Still a good twenty minute walk away. Maybe more like half an hour, considering my blisters. But closer than Etobicoke. And it might be a good place to wait until the power comes on. There might be pay phones! And water fountains! My throat ached. Every time I thought about water, I felt worse. I should get going.

But it was comfortable in the shade. I peered up at the big ivy-coated pile of bricks behind me, bedecked in the gingerbread that characterized a Victorian-built residence, when an idea tapped me on the shoulder. There wasn't a proper yard out front because the house sat so close to the road, but there'd be a back yard. Maybe with a garden. And they didn't have garages, they had little laneways between them. And often in little laneways...

I crawled across the grassy verge on my knees, since my tights were ruined away, and peered around the corner of the house. A coiled hose sat mounted on the wall about two meters from the tall wooden fencing.

I checked the darkened windows to see if anyone was watching; I mean, it's technically private property. Not everyone was suddenly going to grow generous during a time of hardship.

Feeling odd and much more circumspect than I had been when I was cutting the line at the TTC or directing traffic on the Danforth, I tiptoed up the laneway and crouched by the garden hose. I wasn't sure if there would be enough pressure to spray but there should be at least some in the tubing.

When I turned the little tap in the brick wall, nothing came out; I was puzzled for a moment before discovering a secondary tap in the brass nozzle. When I turned it, water spurted freely. Delighted, I stuck my face in the stream. Hot at first, vaguely rubbery, but water. And there was pressure. I drank greedily until my stomach cramped in protest, and then dunked my head under the now cold, blissful torrent, soaking my head and shoulders.

Sated, for the moment, I turned off the hose and rested, enjoying the freedom from thirst. The water soaked through my shirt and blazer and trickled down my back into my skirt. But it was far-and-away better than being itchy with sweat.

Twisting my shoulders to try and distribute the drips better, I happened to see movement out of the corner of my eye and found a tiny, round face peering over the wooden fencing. A little blonde girl, with a smudge of freckles across her nose. I gave her a smile and carefully wound the hose back on its holster.

She continued to stare at me with wide eyes. I gave her a wink and put my finger to my lips. *Just our little secret, eh, kid? You sure are cute—*

The little girl smiled back, then turned and in a volume loud enough to be heard in Scarborough yelled: "MOOOOOM! THERE'S SOMEONE DRINKING OUT OF THE HOSE IN THE DRIVEWAY AGAIN!"

Didn't have to tell me twice. That wasn't a conversation I wanted to have, given how the day had gone so far. On my feet in an instant, I skittered down the laneway, crossing the street and hurrying on my way, blisters throbbing but throat mercifully soothed.

I decided to skip Bloor. It was obvious enough that

power wasn't back on, at least not yet around here; I didn't need to peer into Spadina Station to verify it. And the side-streets of the Annex were so leafy and shady.

My face itched and I resisted the urge to scratch at it, knowing how much it would hurt. Wet rat tails of hair bounced into my face and I stopped to squeeze some of the water out with my fingers. I may have overdone it with the hose but it had been so refreshing. Nearby, someone had set a sprinkler on a lawn, one of those mechanical ones that used water-pressure to sweep the frame back and forth in slow arcs. Children of a variety of ages played together under the water, while the adults hung out on a front porch chatting.

It reminded me a bit of being a kid back in a small town. We didn't have air-conditioning in our old, rambling farmhouse; we had a back porch and huge maple trees with shade, and a pool. I had fond memories of that pool. (My best friend and I had once practised handstands underwater for an entire afternoon. We got quite good at them. But when it was time to get out and dry off for dinner, we discovered that while we'd carefully applied sunscreen to our faces, arms, and shoulders, we hadn't thought about the cumulative effect of that much sun on the soles of our feet. It hurt to walk for several days afterwards.)

That memory reminded my toes that they were blistered and required attention, so I paused to lean against a tree, taking off my pumps and giving my toes and the ball of each foot a rub. Miles to go yet. The idea of waiting until power came back on in Christie Pits—with or without access to the pool—became all that more attractive. Except I wouldn't want to spend the night in Christie Pits. The mosquitoes alone would finish me off, never mind any lurking perverts. (I assume there are lurking perverts in Christie Pits; I mean, that's where I would chose to lurk, if I was so inclined. In fact, that's where I *was* intending to lurk, pervert or not.)

I got a tickle on the back of my neck and glanced over my shoulder, back towards the kids. One of the adults on the porch was watching me. I squinted, wondering if I knew him, but he didn't look familiar; I smiled and gave a little wave hello, just to say, hi, I see you too; but he didn't return the wave and the smile he gave was quite forced. It was a 'time to move along now' smile.

Confused by his hostility, I realized I was hanging out by a tree near a bunch of frolicking kids in bathing outfits while thinking about perverts (not that he could have known *that*. I assume). But I was on my own and bedraggled in ripped and weirdly-soaking clothing.

Giving the Concerned Parent In A Nice Neighbourhood an 'I'm going, I'm going' hands-up wave, I replaced my shoes and continued walking. The old houses and big trees looked less inviting now; more suspicious.

And that made me a little sad.

8.
ISLAND GETAWAY

I don't know how long I walked. The side streets all resembled each other, all Victorian semidetacheds and the odd ugly infill and a little parkette and a convenience store as though each block had a minimum requirement to meet. The heat hadn't diminished; humidity hung in the air like heavy velour curtains from the 70s, the kind that gathered dust unless they were cleaned regularly, which they never are. Back guest room curtains. The ones in hideous shades of mustard and burgundy.

It was very warm and I was very tired.

The humidity kept my hair from drying even as the heat of the day remained, until my head felt like it was wrapped in a wet, warm towel. My feet ached and my thirst-aching throat returned, bringing with it stomach cramps of hunger.

All I wanted was to be at home, feet up, watching my delicious boyfriend making a delicious meal with extra flair and pan-flipping. Dylan was probably worried sick; I still hadn't encountered a working pay phone. There never seemed to be one around when you needed one.

My cell phone hung heavy in my pocket, like a hand-sized rock for all the good it did me. But I did have that one bar of battery left. If I needed it, I could call. But then what if I needed that bar to call a cab? Or an ambulance? Better to wait and find a pay phone. Better to wait and see if the power came back on. It had already been a few hours. How many hours? I wasn't sure. That taxi driver had my watch, wherever he was now, the bastard.

It was very hot.

Dylan had likely already eaten. With the refrigerator out of power, it's not like he could store the dinner for when I got in. Or reheat it after. Come to think of it, the stove is electric. Isn't it? I mean, his is gas. But it has electric components? The pilot light? I have no idea how gas stoves work. I'd never thought about them before.

I hadn't eaten since before the presentation. There had been sandwiches out on the long tables but Aggie and I didn't touch them. There was an unspoken rule that they were for clients, although I am fairly sure I saw John sneak one. But then he would. He was probably at his cottage already, sitting on a dock somewhere, watching, I dunno, loons fishing or something. Beavers? I had no idea where his cottage was, or whether it was on a lake or a river or in the middle of woods somewhere. Did people have cottages not near water? But then how would you go swimming?

(Wasn't swimming the point of having a cottage? Swimming, barbequing, and then a real bed? A proper bathroom so it wasn't camping. Somewhere with a couch and board games that were missing pieces and a macrame owl. Cottages always have a macrame owl hanging on a wall; it's the law. That's how you know the cottage is ripe and ready for harvest: it has grown a macrame owl.)

The patterns of leaves overhead made a soothing blend of light and dark, rippling along the cloudless sky. Leaves on a pond. No, that's not right. If they were leaves on a pond and I was looking up at them, wouldn't that mean I was at the bottom of the pond?

It would be so cool, and dark.

John was probably right now at the barbeque, beer in one hand, funny apron donned. Fucking John and his fucking cottage.

My stomach growled.

I emerged from the shady side streets onto a bigger road, delighting in a bit of a breeze. Not much. But the movement lifted some of the heat out of my still-sopping hair and carried it away until I grew lighter, and dizzier.

Where was I?

More to the point, where was everyone else? There were no cars on the road. I didn't recognize any of the stores and I couldn't find a street sign. *Must be Ossington*, I decided, based on no evidence at all except how tired I was from walking. Across the tops of two- and three-storey shops the sky darkened, banding in purples and reds, marking west; making Bloor south, to my left.

It was eerie without any people walking around. Everywhere else there had been people out and about, living their ordinary lives or walking home like I was. And now there was no one, not even at windows or at doors. The storefronts were cutouts of black. Perhaps it was the cooler air, or the sudden sight of the sunset, but goosebumps rose on my neck and arms, even inside my jacket.

I'm not a praying person. My feeling is that if I leave well enough alone, *I* will be left well enough alone. Not a scientific mode of thinking, I admit, but the idea of 'don't start none, won't be none' lay at the core of whatever scraps formed my philosophy. Of course, I didn't always follow that, but then everyone is a hypocrite, from time to time.

My point, dizzy rambling aside, is that even an apathetic non-believer like myself can recognize when certain boundaries have been crossed. And lacking another explanation... after all, only a few blocks behind me, streets rang noisily full of kids playing, and now the city was deserted. Lifeless asphalt and empty trees. There weren't even any pigeons. Why weren't there any pigeons?

I wasn't on Ossington, I was on Bathurst. I discovered this at the next intersection, Barton, which had a sign-post half-ripped from its pole and bent in the middle. Were those tooth marks? Oddly mangled sign aside, at least I knew where I was, feeling foolish for forgetting that Bathurst came before Ossington when heading westbound. I wasn't sure how far Barton was from Bloor, not being overly familiar with the Annex, but it couldn't be that far.

And then my nose caught a scent.

Hot dogs. Someone had a food cart! Those were propane-powered, not electric!

Once of the first things I'd eaten during my inaugural childhood visit to Toronto was 'streetmeat', as it was affectionately named to me. The hot dogs are of proper and generous size, not tiny like ones you'd buy at a supermarket. Not like the tasteless disappointments I had during a school trip to New York (mind you, New York redeemed itself with delis later the same day). And instead of bland, insipid condiments, Toronto streetmeat could be dressed like a queen: honey mustard, spicy ketchup, corn relish. Olives! Pickles! Bacon bits! All proper vendors had a buffet of condiment tubs attached to their cart. And toasted buns. It was the best thing to eat after getting out of a bar or a club in the wee hours. (Very often the *only* thing, but that does not detract from its glories.)

The scent was thin, a whisper of a vapour against a large and uncaring city, but it could have been trace elements three atoms wide and I would have followed it. I became a bloodhound. My blisters stopped throbbing, my head stopped spinning—everything in my being, each coiled strand of DNA within each cell, now had a singular intention: to find food. I would track that hot dog vendor to the ends of the Earth and load that streetmeat up with every single available option until it was more condiment than bun, and then I was going to—

—shit. I'd have to pay him. I had no money. And that fucking taxi-driving backstabber had my watch. Necklace? It was cheap and not sentimental; it would do for bargaining. I didn't wear any rings, and the ones I had at home were heirlooms. Also: they were at home. Not a point that could be ignored. Necklace it would have to be.

My cell phone weighed me down like a boulder, but no. First, it wasn't mine, it was eSaleEase's; and secondly no. I'd lost my purse and presentation case, my watch and my wallet: I wasn't going to lose my cell phone.

Assuming the vendor would be in front of Bathurst Station—that's certainly where I would set up shop, given the option—I quickened my pace south, but as the subway station appeared in front of me, it sat as deserted as the street. More so, for there were streetcars half in the rail loop, frozen, dark, and empty. Left where where they had stopped working when the overhead power-lines shut off.

The doors were unlocked, so I walked in, but no one was in the station, not even to turn people away. So early? It was still late afternoon. Evening? The sun sat where I had left it, hidden behind buildings but still lighting the bottom half of the sky. Even the colours hadn't changed, like a painted backdrop to a movie set.

There may not have been transit service but there was something nearly as good: pay phones. A whole bank of pay phones! I grabbed the first one eagerly. I could reverse the charges or something. Call collect.

Except there was no dial tone. "Hello?" I jiggled the little tongue that the receiver rested on. "Hello? Can anyone hear me?"

"Hello?" replied a small whisper back out of the machine.

"Hello? Are you with the phone company?" I asked, holding the handset with two hands, as though afraid it would fly away.

"Phone company? No. Who is this?"

"My name's Mallory. I need to call my boyfriend but I don't have any money."

"The phone won't work without money," said the tiny voice, in a soft sigh, almost like a flutter of wings. Soft, feathery wings. Why was I thinking of wings?

"Can't I collect call?"

"Oh, I don't think so. Collect calls? You'd have to catch them first." Tiny, cooing laughter, then the same whispery sigh. "Can I help you with anything else?"

My throat caught. "I'm really hungry," I whispered. "And thirsty, and tired."

"Oh, I can't help with that either," the voice replied, sadly. Then: "What's your boyfriend's name?"

"Dylan. Dylan Mareca." I clutched at the receiver and thought about the comfort of the apartment over the health food store, of the tiny patio at the back, the cluttered bookcases and photograph frames covering the mantle of the unusable fireplace. "He lives in Islington Village. I was supposed to get home. He was making me a special dinner. But it's probably too late now."

"Oh, dinner," cooed the voice. "That sounds lovely. What was he going to make?"

"A surprise." I lamented.

"How wonderful. Surprise dinner. And then would he dance for you?"

"...what?" I pulled the handset away to regard it as though I would see something besides ordinary black plastic. I gave it a shake and placed it back to my ear.

"You should only pay attention if he dances for you," continued the voice. "Otherwise, how will you know he's healthy?" A pause, and the same dry rustling. "I have to go. She says that she's ready to see you now."

Then came silence, a deeper absence of dial tone than just a broken phone, and I knew the voice was gone. I replaced the handset, and out of curiosity sought out the coin return. I pulled out something too small to be a quarter—a dime perhaps?

No. Better: a TTC token.

I tucked the little aluminum token in my pocket beside my cell phone. I could trade the token for a hot dog; they were about the same price. Maybe the token and the necklace if the vendor decided to be an asshole.

As if my thoughts summoned it, the smell of hot dogs drifted towards me with the breeze, stronger now, and lingering, like a finger lovingly traced along my face. I left the odd pay phones behind and wandered out into the street.

Kitty-corner to the station lay a streetcar, sad and abandoned. And beyond that stood the intersection of Bloor West and Bathurst, the south-west corner being the bulk of Honest Ed's department store, dominated by its oversized marquee sign in red and yellow. What should have been three storeys of light bulbs and sale signs with bad puns ('Is Honest Ed a squirrel? Because these prices are nuts!') in wide, 60s-style marker calligraphy instead stood dark and empty, the mannequins and displays of housewares in deep shadow, the signs barely legible.

The doors of this streetcar were open where the others had been closed. I patted its red flank like a trusty horse and peered around the intersection. With night falling—eventually, once the sun moved again—I wouldn't want to be in Christie Pits, but it could be cool enough to walk the rest of the way. A long walk, an exhausting, miserable walk, but doable. Faster if there were no cars and traffic lights to slow my progress.

And then Honest Ed's lit up.

First came an audible grinding of switches being thrown, and then the banks of yellow incandescent bulbs began to glow, quickly brightening into dazzling glare, before moving through their routine of flashing and flickering like the world's most garish movie marquee.

Excitement surged through me. The power was back on! The power—but all the other buildings remained dark, and there was still no one around. I looked either way along Bloor, but nothing indicated anyone but Honest Ed's had electricity.

I wandered into the middle of the intersection. No cars in either direction, still no sign of life. And the store windows of Honest Ed's remained dark, as if it was closed, reflections and glare dancing across the panes. The sun remained fixed against the sky, I could see a corner of it between two buildings. It seemed less distinct, less real, than the immense sign before me.

What else could I do? I followed my nose.

Honest Ed's Department Store—an institution in Toronto—was an entire square block of kitsch. Open since the 70s?—50s? The Big Bang?—it sold all manner of household items, from cheap clothing to cheap groceries and cheap electronics. I hadn't shopped there in years, once I outgrew the 'fake ironic plaster Elvis bust' decoration stage of my university days (Honest Ed's was held together by dust, memories, and off-brand items), and while the goods stacked in the windows had updated slightly since the early 90s, nothing else had. Even the cheesy Elvis busts looked the same, staring out at me with blank and wall-eyed expressions.

The enormous sign sparkled and danced. Someone had refurnished the sign: normally many of the lightbulbs were burnt out. Not tonight. Tonight it was a glorious beacon to bargains.

One of the entrances was open. Sitting on the deserted sidewalk was a sandwich board with an arrow pointed toward the door. I hesitated—until the smell of grilling meat hit me once again. I stepped through and up the first few steps to the main floor.

Miniature lights were strung across the ceiling, criss-crossing in lazy sagging cords, the bulbs dangling and drifting and competing with the mirrors and faded signage advertising bargains. I walked through the deserted first floor, winding through the white-painted wood and Formica displays and counters of my youth.

Upstairs was usually ladies' wear, but not tonight.

Tonight it became a party space, overflowing with people: all ages, shapes, heights, ethnicities, fashion sense. For a moment I wondered if *here* was where everyone had been hiding, but the room wasn't enough to hold an entire neighbourhood and anyway, nothing yet had explained the weird voice on the phone or the sun not moving. Laughter bubbled up and flowed around me like a spring. After the strained silence of the deserted stretch of city, hearing people was being fed a meal after not eating all day.

But you know what's even better than that? Actually being fed a meal after not eating all day.

Lining the walls, instead of displays and mannequins, were food stands: streetmeat, yes, but also Thai noodles and steamy dim sum… and cheesecake? Pizza? Every time a knot of people blocked my view, the vendors seemed to change. Korean BBQ. Tacos. Tiny doughnuts. Burritos. Roti. My mouth watered, but the crowd was too thick to move. Everyone seemed to have a red or clear plastic cup, but I didn't see where the drinks were stationed.

The dizziness that had followed me since Barton intensified. The room seemed to tilt, although that could have been the floors of Honest Ed's; it was never particularly level. Taking a deep breath, I held my head, and tried to think. All I had to pay for anything was a token and a cheap necklace from the mall. I had to be smart about what I tried to bargain for, and what had brought me here was hot dogs. My original vision was streetmeat swimming in every variety of gooeyness that the vendor cared to provide, and through all the chatting and laughing heads, the hot dog vendor stayed clear. I strode up to him; no one else was in line. "Hi."

The man behind the stall regarded me with curiosity and also a bristling gray handlebar moustache, which seemed overly large and perhaps fake. He sniffed at the air and then slammed his tongs down against the metal counter with a loud clang.

The conversation suddenly ceased as though cut with the gesture. Silence. Everyone watched us.

"You don't have any money!" the man barked, suddenly thrusting a finger at me.

So many eyes on me.

I froze, taking a moment to find my voice. Licking my lips, I fumbled for the token. "I don't, no. But I have a token. I can trade that?" There seemed little point in pretending otherwise.

The man cocked his head at me, sniffing again as I held out the token, then recoiled. "I can't take that! That's not for me!"

I pulled my hand back, fingers tight around the small circle, the heat rising in my face. "I'm sorry, I don't have any other money. My wallet was stolen."

"I can't take that!" the man growled at me again, crossing his arms. Around us, the party began to wind up as if in slow-motion before returning to its initial gaiety and volume.

A hand clamped down on my shoulder. "You'd better come with me," a large, beefy man declared in a Caribbean accent.

"I didn't do anything," I squeaked. He bent down to put his face near mine, then snorted, his nose wet. I recoiled. He straightened, shook his head, and propelled me through the crowd. His heavy hand on my shoulder didn't hurt, but pushed with a lot of strength behind it, making it easier to walk than be shoved.

The party-goers split and stepped away from me, clearing a path towards the far end of the room, under the thickest cluster of fairy lights.

Reclining in a chaise longue under a patio umbrella lay a woman in a pink satin dress from the 50s, the kind with a narrow skirt and bodice and flaps over the hips. She even had on a matching jacket and white gloves. The pink was a very garish choice on the face of it but it made her brown skin luminous and she seemed to glow in the soft light of multicoloured incandescence. She lifted big tortoiseshell sunglasses to peer at me under long false eyelashes. "You crashed my party."

"Oh." I stepped back, bumping into the overly large bouncer standing behind me with his arms crossed. "I'm sorry, I didn't know."

"You didn't know it was a party or you didn't know it was mine?" She handed her drink to one of the many admirers gathered around.

"Both." I pointed back towards the staircase. Only the staircase wasn't where I thought it was. I blinked, then returned my attention to the hostess. "I saw the sandwich board on the sidewalk. I thought it was..." The way she stared at me was off-putting, making me feel small and awkward. Mousy. I licked my lips. "I thought maybe it was Honest Ed's' party? Like a public thing. Because..."

"Because?" she prompted.

"Because of the power outage? Like a community thing?" Honest Ed's was known for its donations at Thanksgiving (free turkeys!) and it wasn't impossible that it had opened its doors during a blackout, but my reasoning sounded hollow, even to me.

She accepted a hand from an admirer, who pulled her to her feet. In her heels she towered over me. "I'm not talking about *here*, honey. Not the building. I'm talking about *here*, my island." She stood waiting, hands on her hips.

I racked my tired, thirsty brain. "...island?" I squeaked.

Each movement, slight or large, that she made was calculated, as though a model on a catwalk. And yet her eyes never left me. Finally she reached out with a gloved hand to gently take my chin in her thumb and first knuckle, adjusting my face this way and that, as if judging my own use in a photoshoot. "Do you realize how sunburned you are, honey?"

"Very," I agreed, weakly.

"Hmm." She let go and sashayed back to her chair to recline. She clapped her hands once and someone sidled up to her, a beautiful and lithe young man with bright green eyes, pointed, like a cat's. "Go get her a drink." She paused, thinking. Then: "And some aloe vera."

He nodded before slinking off, disappearing among the partiers who resumed their conversations, laughter filling the space. The woman patted the camping chair next to her. I glanced up at my beefy guide for permission, and when he nodded, arms still crossed, I sank into the chair gratefully. A sigh must have escaped my lips.

"Long day, I expect. Still doesn't explain why you're here, of course." She took a sip from her drink, ruby lips artfully pursed around a coiled straw. She alone had a proper glass, drinking something that bubbled and fizzed, beads of condensation sliding down under her gloved fingers.

My throat felt like I'd tried to swallow razor blades, and I tried not to show my thirst. "I walked here. From Spadina. Well, north of Spadina." I explained how the taxi driver at Kennedy had agreed and taken my watch before suddenly dumping me by the side of the road, and the car full of students who had driven me as far as Avenue Road before I was forced to part ways.

She listened politely.

"I really didn't mean to crash your party," I finished. "I just... it's been a weird, weird day and I haven't been thinking too clearly."

"Hmm." She gestured behind me. The feline young man had returned, bearing a glass of fizzy drink like the woman's—also in a proper glass, not a plastic cup—and a small squeeze bottle. "I said aloe vera," she chided.

He shrugged and proffered the items to me again, the Honest Ed's price sticker still on the off-off-brand container of lotion, and I took them. "No aloe. But it's for sunburns, so it's the same, isn't it?"

"I suppose." The woman stared at me over her shoulder. "Well? Go on, honey."

I squeezed some greenish, translucent gel into my palm and gently dabbed my face with it. I really preferred to have the drink first, but the way she watched me seemed to speak against it. Wherever I dabbed on my face felt instantly cooler and I sighed again. "Thank you."

"You're welcome. You're my guest." She tapped her fingers as if trying to remember something. "What were you trying to pay with, anyway?"

"A token?" I took a sip of the fizzy drink. It was a blend of flavours that rolled in sequence over my tongue, almost too fast to identify. Coconut. Raspberry? No, cherry. Lime. A savoury hint—basil? Refreshing, whatever it was, and I closed my eyes to enjoy the bliss of sitting down with a cold drink.

If it wasn't for the close-pressed laughter and the smell of humanity, I could almost imagine myself at home on the patio. Poor Dylan. He was probably frantic with worry. I opened my eyes again. "Do you...

do you have a phone I could borrow? My boyfriend—"

But the woman was already waving the question away. "No phones here. We're not connected that way to the mainland, you see."

"Uh... oh." That made no sense at all and it reminded me of the pay phones outside of Bathurst station. "I guess."

"It works whether you think it does or not." The woman replaced her sunglasses as she leaned back, as if she was under full sun, and not dangling Christmas tree lights. "Just like that *embargo* you're under."

"Embargo?" I nearly choked on my drink, dribbling down my shirt. She watched me over the top of her sunglasses as I patted the stain dry. Less wet. "What embargo? What are you talking about?"

"I can't say that for sure, only that you've got one. Must be how you got in here; normally you shouldn't be able to cross the channel." Her nose twitched. "Loopholes crop up no matter how careful you think you're being." She regarded me again out of the side of her long-lashed eyes. "Hungry?"

I didn't have to answer: my stomach growled loud enough to speak for me.

She laughed, showing many too-perfect white teeth. "Of course you are, aren't you. Here." She pulled off one of her gloves, revealing long, well-manicured fingers in an exquisite red polish, which didn't surprise me. She held out the glove, urging it. "You show this to any of the vendors and they'll give you something to eat."

I held the glove delicately. "But I don't have any money..."

"No one does on my island, honey." She once again replaced her glasses and leaned back, sipping her drink. "I trade in favours, not cash. So all that happens is you'll owe me another one, that's all."

My stomach did a flip-flop. "Thank you," I whispered, but I felt sick. Owe her *another* one? I didn't realize she was keeping tabs.

The large beefy gentlemen cleared his throat. I stood, and before I could even adjust my skirt the chair was whipped away by the green-eyed boy who folded it with a loud *clack*.

I still had my drink. That was at least a plus.

I wasn't followed as I made my way through the party-goers, nor did they part for me. I chose a slow meander sideways and carefully through a maze of elbows and gesticulations. Inside, my stomach clenched, either from the food smells or the debt, I couldn't tell you. Mother always warned me about accepting gifts from strangers, since you never knew who those strangers might be, but I'd been so hungry and so tired. And now look what had happened.

As I neared the food tables I debated my wide range of choices. But the hot dog vendor with the big must-be-fake moustache was eyeing me again as if I was about to snatch something precious from under his nose. The thought of being able to present him with a glove that he'd have to honour—as weird as that thought was—outweighed my indecision.

I strode over. Attempted to stride over: someone stepped in my way.

A white guy, a bit taller than me, the kind who is too blonde to be real, with a week's worth of scruff and skiing sunglasses in the middle of summer in downtown Toronto. At night. He probably wore cargo pants. I tried to step around him but he blocked my way, all the while staring over my shoulder and sipping from his red plastic cup. He carried himself like he was still proud of winning beer pong that one time back in college when the hot girl was watching.

I took a deep breath and counted to ten. Well, five. "I'd like to get by—"

He shook his head. "No you don't, Mallory."

I froze; I hadn't told anyone at the party my name. I squinted. "Do I know you?"

"Not yet, no," he replied, taking a drink and nodding towards my own cup. His voice dropped, low, almost inaudible. "Keep drinking. Pretend you're having a good time."

I became aware of people regarding me out of the corners of their eyes. I took another sip of my strange cocktail. More of that hint of herbaceous. Rosemary? It was smothered in something tart, citrus. "Who are you?"

"Doesn't matter," he said, smiling broadly like I'd said something funny. "You don't belong here."

I swallowed, forcing the liquid down. "I'm aware of that," I replied. "But needs must—"

He laughed, showing teeth, and then chugged his drink, crumpling the cup up with one hand, slipping the other around my waist. I tried to pull away and he leaned in, whispering. "Play along."

"Why?"

"Because I'm going to get you home to Dylan," he replied, whispering close to my ear. But there was a tickle missing: he had no breath. "I'm here to help, Mallory."

Cracks grew in my calm facade. "I was just hungry. I could smell streetmeat. I didn't mean to crash anything. I don't even know where I am."

"I know. But if you use Chantuelle's glove to trade for food, you'll owe her twice."

"...Twice?"

"Once for the after-sun cream, once for food."

"And the drink?"

He shook his head. We ended up in a corner away from everyone, as if we were old friends catching up. "That's just being a good hostess."

"Isn't feeding people just being a good hostess?"

He gave a shrug. "Different parties have different rules."

I swallowed again, the drink now flat and uncomfortable, catching on its way down. "I just want to go home."

"I know. But she's right, you have an embargo on you, I don't know from where. But do what I tell you, and as tempting as it is, just leave the schnauzer and—"

"The what now?"

He gave my waist a little squeeze, which looked friendly from the outside, which I am sure it was meant to be, but it only reinforced how helpless and trapped I felt. "That hot dog guy. Used to be a schnauzer."

I tried to pull away from him. "I don't—"

"It doesn't matter. Just listen. I promise this will help."

I approached the chaise longue, still holding the glove. Beefy stood guard. He glanced down at the glove and the empty glass. "Not hungry?" he asked. A light-hearted question, but it rolled off his tongue like an insult.

"No, I decided I wasn't," I replied carefully.

"Decide again."

"No, I'm really decided—" He took a step towards me and I thrust the empty glass out at him. "Thank you!"

Confused, he took it from me and stepped back.

Chantuelle peered over the frames of her sunglasses at me, and gave her glass to a waiting attendant. "Back already?"

"Thank you for the drink, it was very hospitable of you," I said, by rote.

Her eyes narrowed. She replaced her glasses and sat straight, scanning the crowd. "Who have you been talking to?"

"Nobody here," I replied, truthfully. I had no idea who he was, he hadn't offered a name, and he had disappeared as soon as my back was turned. "I've just been thinking, is all, and I should really be going. But I wanted to say thank you first."

She stared at me, then stood, tugging down and smoothing her tight jacket. "It's very rude to just eat and leave."

I held up the glove and gave it a waggle. "I didn't eat. Thank you for the drink." I turned on my heel, took a deep breath, and started through the crowd.

"Wait!"

I looked over my shoulder.

She sashayed over to me, hands on her hips, one glove still on, and then pointed with her bare hand. "That's mine."

"You gave it to me."

Her eyes narrowed. "I see what you're trying to pull here. Tell your little friend, whoever they are, that it won't work."

"No friends here, I'm at the wrong party." Already taller than me, she seemed to grow in height the longer we stared at each other. "I'm sorry for barging in. Thank you for the drink."

"I offered you food and aloe—after-sun care," she sniffed. One of the strings of lights flickered and died, a bulb shattering. "I say when you can leave."

"I haven't eaten, and I didn't know that the lotion was a debt." Off-script, but it seemed appropriate.

"Who's being rude offering contracts without making people aware of it?"

Her nostrils flared with indignation, and then suddenly she relaxed, her face smoothing. She gestured with her bare hand. "This is undignified for both of us. Come, I'll get you another drink, you can have something to eat, and we can talk about that embargo that you're under."

"I thought you didn't know anything about it."

"I don't, honey, but I know someone who might." The *honey* was pure sarcasm but the rest wasn't. Maybe it was the twitch of her shoulders, but she seemed like she wanted to bargain.

"Where would I find them?"

"Can't get there from here, you'll have to take transit," she replied, gesturing back to her chaise longue. The folding lawn-chair had reappeared next to it under the patio umbrella, the crowd clearing a wide path. She gestured like a game show hostess. "Come. I'll tell you all about it."

"No, thank you. I really should be going."

She twitched again. "Just a simple chat."

"No, I mustn't. Thank you again for the drink. A lovely... island you have here." I turned towards where the staircase had been, but it was on a different wall now, and I had to pivot on my heel, pushing through the crowd. The old-timey movie and theatre posters that used to line the walls of the staircase, beckoning to weary shoppers, had changed too. They were all Chantuelle, in various costumes, wigs, and backgrounds.

"Wait! My glove. You have to give it back, it can't go with you," she called, stamping her foot. "You get back here!"

I kept walking. All around me the party-goers' faces

lay in shadow, bestial shapes and angles. A long snout here. Buck teeth there. A flick of an ear. They began to part for me, just as he had said they would, as long as I could see the stairs.

"Give me my glove!" she demanded, her heels clattering on the linoleum. "You can't just take it!"

"And you can't make me owe you for something you offered," I replied smoothly, slowing to a stop to turn around. "Shall we make a deal, even stevens?"

She showed too many teeth, too white and too perfect, then grumbled, and crossed her arms over her satin jacket. "Fine. Glove for directions. Then you leave my island and you don't come back, you understand?"

"Understood." Even if she hadn't made that requirement, it wouldn't have mattered; I had no intention of ever stepping inside Honest Ed's again.

We shook hands on the deal. Her skin was so warm that mine felt cold, even to me, and goosebumps ran along my arms like excited children on the last day of school.

I gave her the glove, and she turned on her stiletto heel, her back to me, her arms crossed. Her feet tapped her impatience.

A thick hand on my shoulder. I shrugged it off. "I know the way."

"I know that," the bodyguard replied, gruffly. "I'm just making sure you go."

The crowd made a rift of space, a tunnel of stares. I kept my eyes straight ahead. The smell of food wafted around me, thick as regret, and my stomach growled and gurgled. I imagined Chantuelle smirked. Perhaps I could feel the smirk.

Finally I reached the staircase. My beefy guide did

not follow, glowering over me as I descended to the lower floor. The air was very warm and heavy, the light bulbs dimming and flickering as I walked underneath. My head swam and it was hard to tell distance. The staircase seemed to go on and on, coiling and coiling. I might have walked a kilometre; it might have been two yards. A few paces. My feet were numb, a blessed relief, but then my hands and fingers grew numb too. I braced myself against a yellowed movie poster, casting Chantuelle in *Cabaret*.

"Keep moving," the bodyguard yelled down.

"I know," I replied, intending a snapped retort but it came out slurred.

The main floor was deserted. The strings of lights were out, the only illumination coming from outside, through the big windows that lined the wall facing Bloor. Yellow and flickering as the marquee danced through its pacing, it was barely enough to outline the corners of displays. I crashed into one, spilling discounted socks. Then another, a cascade of tea cups shattering across the uneven linoleum. I pinballed from one display to another, until I reached the cashiers' desk. I had to slink under the chain that dangled across the aisle, blocking me from the exit. The sign—Next Cashier Please—scraped across my back, the cracked plastic fizzing and hissing.

Five feet to go. The air was as thick as off-brand toffee. The plaster Elvises watched me force myself to the door, head swimming.

The door was unlocked. I stumbled out onto Bloor. The sun was where I had left it against the fake-matte-painting of a sky. I realized all the buildings themselves were cut-outs, like in an old western, props of plywood with no substance behind them. Flat. I looked up at Honest Ed's and it too was painted plywood, the wood grain visible. All except the light bulbs; they were real. Tiny bulbs, flashing their eternal dance. Each one alive. One winked at me.

I slipped off the curb and twisted my ankle, landing in a clatter with outstretched palms. Everything swam around me, colours blurring and smearing. The curb at least felt solid. I took off my shoes. My tights were ruined anyway and there was no broken glass or dog shit in this Potemkin world. Holding my shoes in one hand, I stumbled along the yellow line of Bloor to the streetcar, still half in the intersection, its door open, waiting.

Leaning against the door frame, I asked the driver: "What did you used to be?" My voice still slurred.

She glared down at me, her face in shadow, but clearly appalled at my rudeness—what a question to ask!—and I held up my hands in surrender. "I'm so sorry. That just came out of nowhere. It's been a long day and I had a lot... I had just the one—it was a weird drink." I climbed the steps of the 511 Bathurst streetcar, slightly surprised that it wasn't made of cardboard or scrap wood, like a go-cart.

A cough. I stopped, holding onto a pole for support, looking back. The driver pointed at the fare box.

"Oh right. Sorry. Sorry!" I staggered back, fished the token out of my pocket, sending my phone flying, but I scrabbled and caught it with thick fingers that wouldn't bend. "Sorry!" I deposited the token and the door closed. The driver rang the bell, and the streetcar rumbled into life.

I had never imagined I'd be so relieved to hear a streetcar's familiar *clang*. But such are dreams. Was I dreaming or was I drunk? I couldn't tell. Falling into one of the single seats, I leaned my head against the cold glass. Only this afternoon I'd been on a bus doing the same, and the deja vu was like a thick blanket that draped over my consciousness.

I breathed on the glass and traced a heart in the condensation, with D.M. in the centre, and then I closed my eyes.

9.
DYLAN

You didn't mean the invitation to turn out like this. Camila told their immediate neighbours but she also mentioned it to the landlady and her husband, and they got their wires crossed and thought it was an open invitation to everyone.

Now people you've only met once or twice while getting the mail are on your patio. You're pretty sure that woman in the corner who is setting up candles runs the weird girly health food store next to the actual health food store. To be fair, you haven't gone in; the angel dolls in the window put you off. But she brought candles and the couple who run the health food store brought grass-fed steaks and veganaise-dressed macaroni and they're sharing greens with everyone, even though it's made out of that stuff you're pretty sure decorates salad bars.

Camila brought food that she worried would spoil, and the Aldermans brought theirs too, and everyone's brought drinks. So it's not like you have to worry about feeding anyone. You brought out the potato salad since the mayo worried you most; it was well received.

The bike guy from downstairs is doing his best to chat up Camila while explaining at length why he has all these paper plates left over; you can tell Camila doesn't quite follow, but she's trying to look interested while at the same time catching your eye as you hand a towel to someone you don't know who spilled beer over their shirt.

You take the wet towel back and head inside. Someone is on your couch, nursing their kid; that's not a sight you expected and so you have to do an awkward dance into the kitchen while staring at the ceiling.

Part of you is freaked out by all the people in the apartment, but part of you is enjoying it, too. It's a weird sort of social occasion: it feels like a holiday, only there's no ceremony, etiquette, presents or restrictive traditions. And you can't remember the last time you went to a party where you didn't know a sizable chunk of the people. Maybe school.

Camila's thrown off the bike guy and followed you in. She rests against the kitchen island, unperturbed by the breastfeeding stranger. "Do you know all these people?" she asks, picking a left-over piece of potato chunk out of the bowl.

Mallory hates it when you speak Spanish in front of her, knowing she can't follow anything but the basics. But then, she's not here. "No, I don't," you answer Camila's question, scraping plates off into the garbage. "I am not sure how this happened. But I don't mind."

"It's fun," she agrees, although that's not what you said. "A street party."

"Except in my house."

She laughs, though you didn't mean it to be funny. She's leaning fairly provocatively against the island, that kind of effortless, unaware-of-it sexy, at least until she starts biting at a hangnail. That's less charming.

You go back to scraping plates and clear the sink. "Heard from Carlos?"

"No," she says with a pout. "He's off to visit someone's family in the hills for the weekend, I forget where he said. He's going to call on Monday."

You'd be worried if your fiancée was taking off for rural parts of Ecuador, but she seems nonchalant. "It's only Thursday."

"Takes a day to get there. And there's no phones."

"None?"

She shrugs, then resumes chewing at the hangnail, and you realize she's only pretending to be nonchalant. She *is* worried. But she obviously doesn't want to talk about it, so you don't. Instead you throw her a second towel. "If you're going to hang out in here with me, then you can dry some dishes."

She looks surprised, but catches it, and laughs. "Those that don't work don't eat." She says it in her very slow and accented English and then laughs again. "But in this apartment, maybe it's eat first, work second." She's pleased to be telling jokes in her new language, already tackling the pile of soapy dishes.

Shrieks and playful screams from outside, so you drape the towel over your shoulder and poke your head out the open door.

A pigeon landed on the picnic table before leaping back into the air to dodge flapping hands and flicked paper plates. The pigeon circles around and then lands on the patio railing, near Bike Guy From Downstairs. You could almost swear the pigeon is staring at you, but then, pigeons are too stupid to stare in one direction at once. It coos and ruffles its feathers before settling in. Right there on the railing.

"Think it's rabid?" someone asks, mouth full.

"I don't think birds get rabies," someone else answers. You don't know either of those people.

"That's really gross," a third person chimes in, a person you're vaguely aware of as living nearby. "Maybe it's sick or something? Maybe we should call the animal shelter or something."

"Animal shelters don't care about pigeons."

"Sure they do."

"Not in a blackout. Their phone is probably down. Mine is."

Anyway, things are fine. You head back inside, and the pigeon follows you. It flaps right behind your head, startling you and everyone else, circles the apartment once, and then lands on the sideboard.

"Shoo!" You flap the towel at it. This is all you need, bird shit to clean up. "Shoo! Go back outside!"

The pigeon cocks its head and then very deliberately pokes at a picture frame.

You stop your shooing motions, confused.

It pecks again, delicately. It's a photo of you and Mallory from last summer at a friend's wedding. It's only pecking at Mallory's face, the same spot each time. It's staring at you, you're sure of it, as if it's trying to tell you something.

You step closer, leaning in, when suddenly a towel flies over your shoulder and onto the pigeon, which flaps, stumbles, and falls off the side table in a heap, tangled in the towel. Camila steps past you to scoop the pigeon up, carefully carrying the whole bundle out onto the porch. A flick with one hand to throw the bird into the sky. It falls for a moment then recovers and flies away, disappearing between two buildings, gone from view in a blink.

The party-goers give Camila a cheer and she smiles and winks at you over your shoulder. You slap your towel back over your shoulder and clean up all the junk that fell over in the commotion.

It's silly, but it really does feel like that bird was trying to tell you something. But it's just your imagination. Mallory's probably waiting for the subway to come back on with her coworkers while out on a patio or something.

You set the frame back upright and wash the dishes.

10.
EHARMONY

The *clang* of the streetcar jolted me awake. I sat up, surprised that I'd even been asleep, that the streetcar had moved and I hadn't noticed. I wiped bleary eyes and rubbed my face. The heart on the window was gone, long faded. The lights overhead blinked out, then on; outside was rock face covered with bolted, swooping cables. Rumbling under my feet. Queens Quay terminal?

Union Station. Maybe GO trains were working? I could take one westbound–I didn't have any money–I hadn't gotten a transfer–but I was still inside the TTC system. But I'd have to leave the TTC to get a GO train. The GO was on the honour system, wasn't it? What was more honourable than getting people home in an emergency?

Except I suspected it wouldn't be that easy.

We pulled into a tiled bay along a curved track, nestling against the platform. "Last stop," called out the driver, her voice husky and low, like a blues singer. She got up, changed the sign on the front of the streetcar, and lightly skipped down the steps, obviously expecting me to follow her. Putting my shoes back on, I left via the rear entrance. As I alit the last step onto the tiled platform, the doors shut behind me. We weren't at Queens Quay or Spadina Station. Normally the station name was etched into the walls, but these pale gray tiles were blank. I turned to the woman to ask where we were, but she was gone. I was alone, and the doors of the streetcar were closed behind me.

There was only the one exit, leading to a long hallway covered in more gray tiles. Each careful step of my heels against the ceramic retorted like a shotgun, making me wince. The floor seemed clean enough, so I took my shoes off again, wiggling my toes against the cold freedom.

Overhead fluorescent lights lit the way like daytime. It could be any time. I was underground and I don't know how long I'd slept for. Half an hour to Union usually from Bathurst, assuming normal traffic and frequent stops, and not taking into account coming from another dimension.

Plus, this really didn't look like Queens Quay. There were no signs, emergency intercoms, garbage cans, anything that might be found in a regular TTC station.

The cold tile soothed my feet. I didn't feel thirsty anymore, or, indeed, hungry. My head wasn't swimming, my back didn't itch. I stopped to wiggle my fingers, deliberately testing whether I still had a body: I did.

But I felt nothing. Not even the air on my hands from my breath.

Perhaps that should have been disturbing, but after all the accumulated aches and pains of the day, it was liberating. No longer having mass meant I could pick up my pace, swing my arms and march. I felt great.

The hallway at Queens Quay would have curved to

end in stairs up to Union Station, but this corridor kept straight until it dissolved into a dot on the horizon, all the tiles identical and pristine.

A fluorescent light overhead flickered and died. I tilted my weightless head to look up. A loud buzzing as it flared into life again and I winced, throwing my hand in front of my face.

When I looked back along the corridor, the hallway now ended in a gray door. Stainless steel, with safety glass windows, and the little panels that meant 'push to swing open'.

So I did.

The space beyond was immense, soaring upwards in a coil, a spiral of endless corridor. The coil had no upper limit, instead fading into something akin to daylight, but dimmer. Farther away. The floor was cracked and pitted asphalt and it was covered in plants in tubs. Tall, waving plants in rows, their spiky five-fingered leaves instantly recognizable. Powerful lights were set along the perimeter, hard to look at. I sheltered my eyes with my fingers.

The circulating air was heavy and musky, almost to the point of having a taste. Mindful of my university dorm days, I tried not to breathe too deeply. "Hello?" I called.

Some of the leaves rustled. "About time."

I followed the rustling. A guy about my age, perhaps a bit older or a bit younger: he had the hollow-eyed complexion of someone who doesn't go outside much. Someone who plays a lot of computer games. He snipped at one of the plants, cutting buds. (I assume. I am honestly not an expert in any of this. I simply have friends who are... gardeners. All gardeners talk shop a lot. Even the ones who shouldn't. Honestly, it's not a big deal. Please don't tell my mother.)

He didn't look up from his pruning. There was a small green-and-white ONTARIO GROWS fruit basket slung over his arm.

"Hi," I said, when it became clear it was up to me to start the conversation; only I didn't know what to say.

He regarded me warily, dark bags under his eyes. He looked me over, up, down, and I felt the urge to pirouette. "Not my problem," he decreed, going back to his labours.

"I'm sorry?"

"Probably not enough, to be honest." His nose twitched and he scratched at it. "Can you smell that? There's a male bud in here somewhere. I know it."

"Is that bad?"

"Very. It'll spread pollen and then I'll get *seeds*."

"I thought seeds were a good thing?" I kept my voice light, knowing full well seeds are not a good thing. (Like I mentioned, I have friends who are... enthusiastic. About 'gardening'.)

He sniffed in disdain. "If I was growing strawberries, maybe. As you can see, I already have enough plants. Seeds are useless. And just a hint of pollen'll halt the THC production in a good chunk of my crop."

"Why is that?" I have a good voice for when I want to pretend I'm interested. As I suspected, the man started lecturing, starting at the very basics of plant reproduction while I followed him around the gently waving stalks of cannabis. All that was needed of me were *hmm*s of acknowledgement, supplied at regular intervals, allowing me to keep my eyes and ears open for anything useful.

Eventually, somehow, he found what he was searching for and began to trim away at the plant. "Why not just take it outside?" I asked. "Remove the problem plant entirely?"

He paused in his ministrations to stare at me dolefully. "Because I can't lift the tub by myself. It's too heavy."

I smiled. "Maybe two people can lift it?"

He stared blankly, skeptical. "There's no way to get a grip."

I held up a finger for a pause, then jogged back through the rows to the edge of the curving walls. There was a grate somewhere along here... I'd seen something flapping. There: plastic sheeting caught on the inside of the grate, probably blown off a construction site and sucked in by the fan's intake. A familiar feature of underground parking garages. Wiggling it loose, I bore it back to the gardener, who stared as if at a dead rat.

Crouching at the base of the pot, I folded the scrap of sheeting until it was a couple of layers thick and about as wide as the pot, but twice as long. "Here. Tip the pot up?"

He did, and I shimmied the plastic underneath. "You push," I explained, "and I'll pull. Ready? One, two, three..."

It took a few tries to get the rhythm right, but once we did we could scoot the plant across the asphalt more easily than if we both tried to grip and carry it. He issued directions while I pulled backwards, and together we manoeuvred the male plant out of the row and against the far wall where "they" would dispose of it "later". I didn't ask specifics and none were offered.

"That's good enough," he declared, straightening, stretching his back from being hunched. I didn't hurt at all, since I had no body. "Now the others."

We accrued a line of plants, most in bedraggled stages of hacked-off pruning. "You need help," I said, during a break. "Like an assistant."

"Meh. I'm happier down here on my own. Just me and my plants."

I knew that self-pitying tone. "No girlfriend, huh?"

He bristled. "What do you think? Girls who want to live underground just grow on trees? I'm just going to walk into a bar and find somebody weird like that?"

I sat back on my heels and gave him a frank assessment in return. "That's exactly how you find weirdos, yes, but it's not the only way, and there might be a better solution."

"Oh? I'm all ears."

And so I ended up explaining online dating to someone growing pot in an abandoned parking garage. We sat on wooden lawn chairs—I don't know why so many of the strange encounters I'd had tonight involved patio furniture; perhaps Canadian Tire gives discounts—while he had a beer. I wasn't thirsty. I wasn't anything; it was delightful.

He leaned back, surveying the line-up of plants awaiting disposal, and gave a sigh. "She'd have to like gardening."

"Probably."

"But also not be fond of sunlight."

Vampiric gardeners. They had to exist. Nothing surprised me anymore. "Houseplants. She could be someone who enjoys raising houseplants. Probably also cats."

"Can't stand cats, allergic," he replied, taking a swig of his beer, legs splayed in comfort. He sighed again and rested the bottle of Molson Canadian on the arm of his Muskoka chair. He shifted, then took another swig. "Is that how you met Dylan?"

"No, I met him the old-fashioned way, friend of a friend at a party."

He harrumphed. "Then why are you giving me advice?"

"People tell me stories, I share those experiences, everyone wins." I spread my hands. "Information sets us free."

He harrumphed again. "And this neighbour of yours? Think she's sharing in any experiences?"

I froze. How did he know about Camila? I hadn't told anyone about that.

"Yeah," he continued, smirking. "I thought so."

"It's not like that, I trust Dylan. He's a great boyfriend."

"He'd be a great boyfriend to someone else if you weren't there."

I bristled. "It's not like that!"

He shrugged. "Sure it is. Always has been; always will be. No one is 100% trustable."

The words flew to the tip of my tongue but I bit them back and swallowed them, and *maybe that's why you're alone* rumbled around where my stomach ought to be. "Dylan made me a special dinner," I said instead, as if that was proof of trustworthiness.

"Which you failed to show up for," he pointed out, gesturing towards me with the beer bottle.

"Extenuating circumstances."

"May well be, but that's not going to make any difference. People feel how they feel and facts don't necessarily make a dent in that."

I would have liked to grit my teeth, if I had teeth to grit.

He put the empty down beside his chair and laced his hands behind his head. "Someone who likes houseplants but doesn't like cats."

And who tolerates complete assholes, I silently added.

He looked over at me. "Think that has a chance of

working? Honestly?"

"Sure. There's someone for everyone. Lots of potential someones! You just have to be open-minded to opportunities." I sounded like my mother. "Sometimes, we have to make our own opportunities." So much like my mother.

"Now you sound like a poster with a dolphin on it."

"I work in sales."

"Aha."

"I'm very good at it."

"Sure." He smirked. "So who did you piss off?"

"Pardon?"

His smirk deepened. "You had to have pissed off someone high-up. So what did you do?"

"Nothing?"

He leaned back, smiling out at his rows and rows of plants. "No one ever does, do they?" He pulled out a small cooler from underneath his Muskoka chair. "Well, toots, time to get you moving along again." He opened up the cooler and pulled out a couple of joints. "These might help you remember."

"Uh." Wasn't there a warning about not consuming things—

"It's fine." He knew what I was thinking and urged them at me. "Don't smoke in here, it aggravates my asthma. Take them with you, and when you need it, they'll help shed light on the subject."

I took them carefully. "Are you sure?"

"Call it payment for helping me lift the plants." He snapped the lid closed and slid it back under the chair. "Now you should probably get going. Longer you're here, the colder Dylan's lovely surprise dinner gets."

The elevator doors opened and I stepped out into a

lobby covered in the same smooth gray tiles from earlier. As the doors slid shut behind me, cutting off the tinny muzak rendition of *Hotel California*, I faced a plexiglass-and-steel door on the opposite side of the room. I put my shoes back on. My heels were silent across the tiles.

I pushed open the doors to find myself at a set of steps leading downwards. Not industrial stairs, but narrow ones, covered in brown carpet, the kind that cheaper landlords favour. One side of the narrow staircase was ordinary drywall; the other old, crumbling red brick. Little niches were formed by missing chunks, with small items in each. I found tiny Kinder egg toys, plastic flowers, lumps of nearly spent candles. A crayon. Some pennies.

And then a lighter. I scooped it up, leaving a dime in its place.

A heaviness settled over me with each step downward, like weights tied to my arms and legs. I felt myself inflating, as if I was a pool toy being blown up, fingers popping into substantiality, toes uncurling in my shoes. I gained mass and nerve endings and aches and pains and by the time I reached the last step I was whole again. Real, exhausted, and sore.

Wearily pushing open the squeaking metal door, I stepped out into a late summer's night across from the Bloor Cinema. Cars drove past, people on bikes wove carefully around obstacles, couples strolled along the sidewalk arm in arm. The windows in the buildings lining Bloor street were all dark, as was Honest Ed's one block west at Bathurst. The real Honest Ed's.

The city was still blacked out, but I was back in my Toronto.

And I really needed to pee.

11.
DYLAN

You pause, knife in hand, but then give a shake of your head and slide the utensil along the edge of the lamb roast where it's sticking to the pan. This isn't what you wanted; you wanted to make your girlfriend a special dinner. She knew that. And yet she hadn't shown up. Hadn't even bothered to call.

Most of the neighbours, especially the older ones, and the ones with kids, have gone home already, taking their empty food bowls with them, leaving many of the candles behind. They're stumps now, the candles, sagging into the wood of the patio railing or the picnic table, guttering and smoking, but still light.

Not everyone has gone. Glasses are still being clinked, drained, refilled. There's laughter and goodwill and a sense of community that you hadn't realized you'd missed since you'd left school. You have friends, good ones, but as each of you partner up, marry, have kids, the wedge grows wider and the times when you're all in one room grow farther and farther apart.

Such is life. You knew this would happen. Just like you knew the roast would dry out being in the oven for so long. But part of you hoped for a touch of the miraculous.

You slice the lamb roast. It's dry as leather now, like old boot, but you don't like lamb much anyway so the texture hardly matters. When it was obvious that the power wasn't coming back on in a timely fashion, you took everything out of the fridge for the neighbours, and wrapped an icepack or two around the tzatziki. Still hoping.

But it's not dusk anymore, it's night, and there's still no word from Mallory. Even if she'd *walked* from Scarborough she'd be here by now. So you can only conclude she's staying somewhere. Maybe with her friend Aggie or maybe the whole team is still having drinks and dinner somewhere, waiting for the subway's return.

The last cut. You would have been okay if that's what she'd chosen to do, but she hadn't *called*. And she knew you'd been cooking all day.

You spoon the tzatziki onto the plate out of the container; presentation is still important, even if it is just cold cuts out on the patio. The rich smell of garlic and yogourt and cucumber and mint fills your nose and dampens the lamb. Suzy down in the health food store was right; it's the best sauce to cover up the taste of the meat.

Part of you wants to stop and put the platter back in the fridge, keeping it for when Mallory gets home, but another part of you doubts that will even be tonight. And besides, there are people here, now. Hungry people.

You carry the platter out onto the picnic table to *ooh*s and *ahh*s.

"This smells amazing," calls out Heather, in that annoying sing-song voice that she has, but she doesn't sound like she's lying.

"Dylan's a great cook," Jeff tells her, pulling a piece of lamb onto his paper plate. "The smells that come out of the apartment just when I am getting home, man, it's torture. Why do you do that to me?" But he's teasing, grinning even as he licks a splot of tzatziki from his thumb.

You laugh, enjoying watching people dig in. "I like cooking. It's relaxing, even after a long day."

"See?" Heather digs an elbow into Jeff, as though you've proved a point for her, but you don't know what.

"What do you do?" Jeff's friend Trevor asks, taking a swig of beer. "Besides cook?"

"What else does he need to do?" Heather teases. "God, I love a man who can cook. And you too, I guess, Jeff."

"Thanks."

"I work in banking," you tell Trevor. "It's really boring. Cubicle farm and all that."

"I thought banking was all hot-shot suits and long hours?" You're not sure how many beers he's had; he's developed the troubled-focusing of someone who's been pounding them back.

"Not the kind of work I do." You'd rather not talk about it with him, sensing he's looking for an argument. "I'm out the door on the dot every day at five. Home by 5:30. Gives me time to relax in the evening, and I relax with food."

"Doesn't everyone?" Heather teases. She's awfully teasy tonight, but she's also draped around Jeff like a wet towel.

And then there's Camila. She's still here, still happy to sit with everyone, rarely talking, answering in measured sentences, taking sips from her beer. "Food is important," she says, finally taking a slice of meat. "Food is family. Back home, food is everything. Here, food is fuel. You eat because you're hungry, like a robot."

This pronouncement grinds the conversation to a halt. They're unsure of what to say, whether to correct her or agree or let it slide. She doesn't care; she's moved on, eating the lamb with careful bites and watching you under her eyelashes.

"Who wants more drinks!" you say, getting up, falsely bright and acutely uncomfortable.

There's a chorus of "me pleases!" from around the table, beer-drinkers and water-onlies alike. You scoot out of the picnic table and head back inside, feeling a little dizzy.

Truth is, Camila's right, and it's something that bothers you about Mallory; how she eats like, yes, a car gassing up. Open hatch, insert fuel until tank is full. Keep going. It's not that Mallory isn't appreciative, because you know she is, but she's not appreciative about the *food*, she's appreciative about the *work* because it means she doesn't have to cook unless she feels like it, which is rare. And there's a difference and you've never put it into words.

But Camila did.

There's a few beers left. You sweep them into a convenient box and fill up a pitcher with cold water from the tap. Thank god you've still got water pressure, but then you're only on the second floor. Imagine dealing with this long a blackout without water. Or toilets!

A smell wafts across your nose, heady and musky and herbal. You leave the refilling pitcher to stick your head outside. "Trevor? No thanks, man. I don't want the smell in my apartment."

Trevor stops, confused, pulling the joint away from his lips and examining it, as if the idea of people objecting to the *smell* of weed was something that had never occurred to him. "It's just a joint."

"Come on." Jeff takes it from him and stubs it out on the picnic table, adding to the wood's collection of scars. "Don't be like that."

"Hey! Don't be like what? What's the harm?"

"It's not your house. Don't be uncool."

"I'm not the one being uncool—"

You go back to the sink, hating the tension in your jaw, that familiar clench of teeth. Trevor's going to push back, you know he is, and then you're going to end up asking him to leave, and the mood of the party will be ruined. You turn off the tap. Maybe it's already ruined; it's late anyway. But it's your place, not theirs, and your rules.

The smell drifts by your nose again, this time woven with something floral, almost like a familiar perfume but more natural. You stomp back to the doorway, ready to do battle, but everyone looks up, surprised at your heavy-footed arrival. No one is smoking anything; the joint remains stubbed and charred and Trevor is empty-handed.

But you can still smell it.

You lean over the railing, trying to figure out where it's coming from, but it could be anywhere. Candles don't throw light very far and the buildings block the moon and starlight. Off the patio could be nothing. You're on an island, separate from everything else, marooned with people you didn't invite, without the one person you wanted to spend the evening with, and suddenly you're very tired.

"Maybe it's time we get going," Heather says, stretching.

"No, no," you insist, turning back to them. "There's still lamb left and I found a few beers. The evening's still young."

Heather smiles at you and snuggles up to Jeff, who puts an arm around her. "It *is* nice out here."

"Almost makes you wish we had power-outs more often," someone else jokes. You forget their name, another friend of Heather and Jeff's.

You go inside to get the drinks. The smell is gone and you can't even remember what it reminded you of.

12.
BETWEEN BANJOS AND A HARD PLACE

The last I remember clearly, it was late afternoon while I walked along Barton. After that, my thoughts became hazy and indistinct. At the time I had assumed mild heat stroke; now with the experience of not-having-a-body, I could recognize the experience for what it was, a shifting of boundaries.

As I gazed around a bustling Bloor and Bathurst—cars, bikes, pedestrians, street musicians, dogs, students, was that a rat—I wondered how long I'd been away. The sun was completely gone, and the night air cooler than the furnace of the afternoon, but still warm and humid. It tasted stale.

Even without power, the Annex continued to be lively. The shops were all dark, many of them closed and locked. Windows hung open in the apartments above storefronts, some with candles, some with people leaning on the sill, hanging out for a hope of breeze. At the end of the block, one of the bars had a full patio still pulling in customers.

They'd probably have a bathroom I could use.

The patio tables were covered in assorted candles—

maybe people were bringing their own?—and customers clustered around them, drinking warm beer, wine, ice-cube-less juice and water. Some poor soul dodged around both drunk people and open flames, taking orders and bearing plates of burgers. How were burgers still being cooked?

I tried to catch her attention.

"Just sit anywhere," she said hurriedly without looking at me. "It's not exactly service as usual tonight—"

"Actually, I just need to use the washroom," I clarified, putting on a hopeful face (and trying not to tap dance).

"Oh." She stopped, apologetic, readjusting her tray. "Sorry, hun, no washroom tonight."

"What?" I blinked. "Why would the *toilet* need power?"

"Oh, no, it's not that. The bathroom's down, like, a narrow flight of stairs and a long hallway in the basement, right? I just cracked my forehead a few minutes ago and I've been down that staircase a million times. It's just too dangerous in the dark." She did indeed have a long, thin bruise developing over her eyebrows, which possibly also accounted for her dazed demeanour.

Or it could be the waitressing in the dark.

Someone overheard us. "No bathroom? Isn't that, like, a health code violation or something?"

Their partner across the table laughed. "You're drinking warm beer and eating unrefrigerated meats and you're only caring about the health code *now*?"

"Yeah, but beer can't go off. I mean, it's gone off already. Hasn't it?"

"What's this about the burgers?"

"The burgers are fine."

"How are they even cooking them?"

"It's a *gas stove*, guys."

A gas stove. That made sense—mechanical, right? I had whispers of a memory of Dylan explaining about his gas stove, a cranky monstrosity lurking in the corner of the kitchen. I was forever cranking the heat too high and causing shouts that I'd burn the house down. (To be fair to myself, my heart has never been in cooking. If it was up to me, I'd eat cereal three times a day. It's much more satisfying to watch Dylan cook anyway.)

The conversation continued around me, with each eavesdropping patron offering their own two cents on the pros and cons of having a restaurant open during a blackout, all while the harried waitress tried to bus tables.

Eventually she bustled back into my general vicinity and rolled her eyes at the philosophical discussion, gesturing northwest with her chin. "Try the subway, hun, they might still have their bathrooms open. Most of the bars closed early today. We're only open because my boss is a complete—" She stopped and cleared her throat. "Anyway, don't tempt fate and all that. You're not ordering or anything?"

"No thanks." I tried to smile, but she was already carrying the full tray away. How were they washing dishes? In the dark? That disgusted me more than the potentially undercooked burgers. I don't think I was alone in that concern, since mostly people were drinking out of bottles. It reminded me of the storekeeper giving away perishables and waters. But the people here were still being charged.

Capitalism, I guess. I wondered if the meat was discounted.

"Hey." Someone nudged me. No one I knew; he had a beer in one hand, too much aftershave, and that particular and unwelcome look in his eye. "If you need a washroom, you can come back to my place and use it, babe."

I forced away the urge to make a gagging face. "That's okay, thanks." He stepped closer and I had to back up, smacking into one of the small tables. The occupants, startled, braced it before candles could fall over. "Sorry." I tried to step past him but he stepped in sync, leaning over me.

"Come on, don't be like that, we're having a party," he cajoled with a leer, trying to get a hand on my ass, but before I could knee him in the 'nads (I think we can all agree here that I've had A Day and no longer had any patience to spare on strangers trying to grab me) one of his friends pulled him away, alarmed but trying to laugh it off like 'oh, that's just our creepy friend, ha ha, what a card'. Yeah, ha ha ha, *fuckface*.

Ugh.

I was so tired. I came here to use the bathroom. But I was getting to the point where I was fed up enough to just pee in an alley or behind a bush if I had to. I didn't care anymore. I was half-tempted to pee in front of Creeper just to make a point.

One of Creeper's friends tried to invite me to join them—like I would, after that!—but he was mercifully interrupted by someone shouldering past him bearing a guitar. No, wait. Was that a banjo?

It *was* a banjo. Who plays banjos? Besides cowboys? They didn't look like cowboys, they looked like skinny art students. They were setting up in a corner of the patio while other patrons looked on, as confused as I was.

"Oh, thank god you're here, Tyler," the waitress remarked, arms full. "I called you like two hours ago!"

Phone? My ears pricked up.

"We had to walk, I told you that already, Sandra." Tyler, the first banjoist, tuned his instrument with the serious expression of a put-upon *artiste*. Then he was joined by *another* banjo player. And another. What was this, a convention? I'd gone my entire life without seeing a banjo player before and now there were three of them. Three years into the 21st century and art students play banjos now.

Focus, Mallory. There's a phone on the premises.

I let Sandra pass me and fell into step behind her. She was only half-paying attention, so I grabbed a tower of plates and some glasses—take that, summer working at the Keg, you came in useful after all for more than beer money—and followed her to the kitchen door. She watched me put the plates down in the stacks with the confused face of a dog who doesn't understand where the ball went that you just threw. Like the world had broken.

"You looked like you could use the help," I said, over the din. Behind her, someone was grilling, flames leaping, bright against the dark.

"Thanks," she said, but her face didn't change. Still confused, she went back out and I followed, clearing debris while Tyler and Two More Banjos began twanging merrily away, causing drunken conversations to lurch into wide-eyed silence. If I, tired but sober, was this bewildered by the sudden performance, the drunkards—who were, after all, drinking without eating in many cases—were stupefied.

But they weren't bad, judging by the standards of a student amateur band. I certainly sat through worse in my undergrad days. The song they played sounded oddly familiar but I assumed it was some sort of cowboy tune and didn't pay it much mind while I gathered up more dishes.

"I told you, hon, I can't let you use the bathroom," Sandra said. She'd figured out why I was helping her as I dumped glasses into the sink. "It's, like, terrifying." She gestured at an unlit hallway that stank of old grease and culminated in a staircase straight out of nightmares. "Even Lucas doesn't want to go down there and he's, like, 6 feet of nothing scares Lucas."

I blinked. "It's not that." It was, but who was I to go where Lucases fear to tread? "I was just wondering if I could use your phone to call home? It's not long distance. My boyfriend's probably worried sick." For a half-second I had a flash of what I would do if Camila answered the phone, but she wouldn't do that. I mean, Dylan wouldn't do that to me. I shook my head. "Just for five minutes. I promise to be quick and help you some more, too."

"Aww, hon." Sandra couldn't have been more than 22, but her gravelly voice sounded like my grandmother's next-door neighbour. She wore another doggy expression, the one where they tilt their head and put a paw on your knee because they know that you've had a day with no treats too. She wiped her hands on her apron and rubbed her eyes. "Fuck, I could use a cigarette."

"No smoking!" barked someone from the back of the kitchen, possibly Lucas.

"I know, I know." Sandra sighed and shifted a glance outside.

"I will be super quick," I repeated.

"The phone's dead, hon," she said with a sigh, gesturing to the wall behind me where a portable phone sat at the cash table. "Battery gave out an hour ago."

Fuck. Well, I tried.

We both stood in the door, watching the banjo-jamming art students, and something about the song tugged at my memories like a too-excited child. Someone staggered to their feet, clapping, one of the creepy guy's friends. He was humming along very loudly, and I suddenly recognized the song(s). "Is that... are they playing a medley of Mariah Carey songs?" I scratched at my nose. "On a set of three banjos?"

"We live in mysterious times," Sandra agreed, wearily. "But at least no one's currently bugging me about warm beer or to see a menu they can't read in the dark."

I regarded Sandra with new admiration. "You're getting time and a half for this, right?"

"No," she admitted. She gave me a sly smile. "But the machine's down and I'm having to write all the totals out, on, like, paper. Who knows what sort of mistakes I'll make?" She pulled out a pack of cigarettes and tilted them towards me, but I demurred. "Yeah. You're probably right." But she pulled one out and lit it anyway. She blew out the smoke with heart- and lung-felt sighs. Shouting erupted from the kitchen and she rolled her eyes at me. "What's he going to do anyway? Call the health and safety guys?"

I grinned. "Anyone working tonight deserves *at least* time-and-a-half, I think."

"Me too."

We gave each other a nod of agreement, and she disappeared into the kitchen to trade shouts with someone, possibly six-foot-scared-of-nothing-Lucas, and I drifted out onto the patio.

Drunk Creeper's Pal had migrated next to the trio of art students, taken his t-shirt off—because it was business time, apparently—and twirled it around his head while launching into a very spirited rendition, perfectly timed, of "Fantasy Boyfriend".

The rest of the patio stopped, open-mouthed; Drunk Creeper's Pal had pipes. And a phonographic memory for Mariah Carey lyrics. The three art students shifted from confusion to joy and really shredded... on... the banjos.

Maybe you think that people cannot shred on banjos to Mariah Carey songs.

You would be wrong. And I have seen it.

Someone reached out to touch my wrist and I jumped. The woman startled too, hands up in surrender. We both reflexively said "sorry!" at the same time, and then relaxed, chuckling. "They're not bad," she said, with a head tilt towards the impromptu performance. "It's like Mariah Carey karaoke—"

"MARIAH CAREYOKE," we both finished, laughing. She cheersed me with a beer as the band swung into the next song, which I don't know the name of but I can hum. Drunk Creeper's Pal—now the official Mariah Careyokist—was already starting to lose his voice on the higher notes, but none of his enthusiasm.

"Lee's Palace," the girl said, starting to clap. Everyone was starting to clap.

"What?"

She gave me an awkward smile. "You might want to try Lee's Palace."

I still didn't understand. "For what?"

A friend on at the table was listening in and nodded enthusiastically, adding: "It's open, running, like, open-air acoustic concerts or something? I forget what they called it, but they were standing outside trying to drum up business or whatever."

It took me a moment to grasp what they were trying to tell me. Both looked scarcely older than the kids in the car from earlier in the afternoon. "You think... I can use their bathroom?"

They nodded again with the vigour of the helpful/tipsy. "I know the waitress said to try Bathurst station but that's closed down. Locked. They just gave up. Buses are running out of gas. Shuttle buses, I mean. Or I guess, like, all of them."

"Really?"

More nods.

"I'm kinda enjoying this," one of the girls said, her gesture encompassing half the Annex. "I mean, not the warm beer part, but like, just hanging out and listening to live music and not having to work on my thesis because it's on my computer."

"Oh my god, I didn't even think of that," her friend exclaimed. "I was just slacking but that's totally a better excuse."

"Totally is," I agreed, as the Mariah Careyoke superstar broke off the song to be sick into the potted shrubs, causing Banjo Player #2 to recoil and fall off their stool. "Which way is Lee's Palace again?"

13.
CLASH OF THE ROCK BANDS

I agreed with the slacking student: the break from the ordinary was fun, or at least it would have been if I'd been in a place to enjoy it—say, at home, with Dylan. But the breakdown of infrastructure was less fun when I had no way of getting home and/or a need to pee. I very much hoped I wouldn't have to ruin anyone's shrubbery.

While all the candles and people in windows and live music on open patios was very charming and bohemian, the others were a disheartening sight. The trudgers. The people who had obviously been at this a while and still had miles to go. Many of them were in business casual, their make-up running from sweat, their button-up shirts stained. They took me in as I did them; we were kin. But they had resigned themselves to trudging whereas I remained ever hopeful of an opportunity.

But then—the thought wearily settling over my shoulders like a throw blanket made of stone—if I'd just walked straight from Kennedy I'd probably be getting out to Islington by now.

Buried in my own thoughts as I was, I might have walked right past the multicoloured graffiti'd exterior of the club known as Lee's Palace except for the crowd out front, spilling onto Bloor. The few eastbound cars still on the street diverted into the westbound lane to get around as more and more people gathered.

I hung back to get a lay of the land, then skirted the edge of the crowd towards the door. A couple of guitarists were setting up stools, and someone else fixed up a drum kit; the drunk girls had been right, there was an acoustic concert going on. Which, again, in any other circumstance would have been really cool to be a part of.

But I just wanted a toilet.

Sliding up to the door, I asked the bouncer if I could use the washroom.

"Cover's $10."

Blinking, I stared up at the wall of denim and tattooed muscle, almost as garishly festooned as the walls of the club. "Cover?"

"That's what I said, lady."

The way he called me lady reminded me of Squints and his meaty grip, and I bristled. "Why is there cover if the band is setting up outside, huh?"

Wall o' Meat regarded me impassively. "Because people like you keep wanting to go inside."

"I just need to pee. There's nowhere else open."

"Not my problem."

"It will be your problem," I informed him.

He raised an eyebrow. I either had to back down ASAP or bluff my best. "If you don't let me in, I will pee. Here. Right here."

Another raised eyebrow.

I gritted my teeth. He didn't move. "I just need to pee!"

"Then pay the $10."

Something inside me threatened to snap (and I don't mean my bladder). "Fine! You're going to be the one cleaning the mess up!"

"No I won't."

Someone accidentally elbowed me, and I got pushed out of the way. Not hard, and not maliciously, but enough to break the confrontation with Brick o' Beef. Scowling, I stalked away, temporarily defeated. Psyching myself up to pee behind a dumpster if needs must. I'd already drunk out of a garden hose; it was just a slippery slope.

Turning down the alley, I was surprised to find that the streetlight was on. "Power's back!" I threw out my hands in joy, but as I looked around, I noted that none of the other streetlights or windows were lighting up. Peering in confusion, I realized that the full moon had risen behind the still-broken streetlight.

Glowing like anything, the moon made me both a little surprised and a little saddened over my joy at a lightbulb returning to life. But it was nice to see ol' Luna, and she certainly was bright. Astonishingly so. Strange how it took the whole city going dark for me to notice.

I spotted a row of dumpsters; if there was decent space between any two then that would give some privacy and also I presumed anyone unfortunate enough to be around dumpsters would be used to encountering this sort of thing. Wouldn't they? I didn't want to think about it.

The two furthest dumpsters were the right distance apart but as I walked towards them I heard voices and a door swinging open, and out of instinct I ducked behind a stack of old boxes. Two employees stepped out into the night air, bitching about having to work during the blackout.

I considered asking one of them about their bathroom but as both were bulked-up walls of meat like the bouncer, I suspected that they'd be equally resistant. Especially if I was skulking around in the garbage.

One of them held the door open, since it was one of those self-locking doors, while the other lit their cigarette, the flare from the match startling in its intensity. "Light one for me, will ya?" He gave the door a shake to indicate his less-than-free hands.

"Don't be such a dope," the other replied. While his colleague stared in pained confusion, the smarter of the pair jammed a scrap piece of wood under the door. "See? Now we can get back in. Come on, I want to see the Maytags playing."

"But—"

"Suit yourself, man."

Making sure they were gone, I peered out, deliberated, and then shot to the door. Would you rather pee in a sketchy club toilet or between a pair of smelly restaurant garbage receptacles? Yeah, I thought so.

The hallway led to the kitchen, which was empty, and lit with nothing but moonlight from outside; creepy, but deserted. Hearing voices at the other end of the hall, I decided that should it come to it, I would play dumb and pretend to be with one of the bands. I mean, I was dressed in a dark suit and heels. I could be someone's... agent? Sure. Let's go with that.

I crept along the hall. Bathrooms should be close to the kitchen. Plumbing and all that. Checking each door, I discovered two storage closets before—yes—a tiny, grimy bathroom.

Bliss.

Washing my hands in the dark, I felt around on the wall for a hand-dryer or paper towels but the roller was empty, so I ran my hands over my jacket. I was sweaty enough that my wet hands probably made my jacket cleaner.

Opening the door, I checked the hallway. Clear so far but—shit. The two-legged bricks were back.

"I need to use the bathroom first, okay?" one of them said, the voice lurching closer towards me. I couldn't get out the way I came, so I pressed on, turning the corner, hoping to find a place to wait until the coast was clear to sneak back out.

Instead, the voices kept a steady pace behind me, driving me further on. Each door I tried was locked until the last. Swinging it open, I found myself at the stage. More voices up ahead. The hallway was dark, the backstage area was darker—no windows—but a red glow up ahead—one of those emergency signs that runs on batteries. Yes! An exit. If I could just get to it—

I bumped into someone.

"Hey, watch it."

With sinking horror I realized that I wasn't alone in the dark corridor. "Sorry!" I said brightly. "I couldn't see you."

"Yeah, no kidding."

"Wait, is that you, Rachel?"

"Nooo, I'm Mallory," I corrected quickly, trying to use the painfully small amount of light from the distant emergency exit sign to figure out how to get past an unknown number of people. "But I can tell Rachel you're looking for her?"

"Hey, wait," someone said to one of the others, in a quieter voice. "Wasn't Mallory the name of the manager for the Maytags?"

Have you ever had that experience where you know

someone's looking at you and the hairs on your neck and arms all stand up at once? I swallowed. "That's right, that's me," I said, brightly. Who the fuck were the Maytags? Probably the band outside. "I just came back in to—"

"Yeah, we don't care, okay, lady?" Someone sounded irritated. "We just found out that you and your stupid fucking band were double-booked with us and now they're not going to let us play, right? And we came from really far for this gig and there's no fucking power."

Assorted grumblings agreed with the speaker.

"Sorry?" I said, with a rising intonation, trying to slide along the wall. "There must have been some sort of mistake. I had no idea you were booked as well." The grumblings didn't subside and I figured, why not go for it. "Who are you guys?"

"We're called Straight Messina," someone announced proudly. "We're the first metal-ska-funk band in the GTA. Maybe, like, ever."

"Wow," I said, with the most enthusiasm I've ever tried to muster. It was then that the door opened in the distance and a large, bulky shape entered. Shit. The first bouncer. He'd definitely recognize me if he heard me and he could palm my head like a basketball. "Where are you fellas from?"

"We're not all guys, okay?"

"Very sorry about that. Can't see a thing." I squeezed between two of them. Worse yet, the two smokers from the back door had come around the corner. Now there were three sides of meat to avoid. How many bouncers did one club need, anyway? Conversationally, but lowering my voice, I asked: "Where did you say were coming in from again?"

"Brampton," someone replied, sulkily.

"That's pretty far," I agreed. "Excuse me, sorry."

"Where are you trying to get to, lady?"

Obviously I couldn't answer the truth: 'trying to put you between me and those bouncers who can palm my head like a basketball' so I went with: "Trying to get out of your way, of course. So you can continue setting up."

There were scufflings and weird rattlings as they turned to follow my voice.

"...setting up? But we're double-booked, remember...?"

"I know. But... but it's hardly an ordinary night, is it? What did you say you played again? Metal and what?"

"Ska-funk."

"That sounds like a super combo. Really... original. Do you have representation?" The bouncers were close and one of them shouted in a temper at the others about the crowd outside. "No? I would give you my card but they're... in my other suit. In my car. In the meantime, fell—uh, people, I'd really love to hear what you're made of."

"But there's no power?"

"Right. Which is why... this is such a great opportunity for you. Because anyone can sound good with amps and, you know, microphones, but it takes truly great performers to... perform... regardless of a blackout or not. The show must go on, right?"

More rustling and some whispering. "The Maytags are outside," someone reminded us, the question hanging in their voice.

"True, but it's a free country and Bloor Street has two sides." The bouncers were coming over. Gritting my teeth, I tried to crouch down so that I blended in with the others, who smelled liked old wigs and grease paint.

"Hey, who's here? What are you doing back here?" Wall o' Meat demanded.

"We're Straight Messina," the first voice said, indignant. "We were booked by management. We're supposed to be playing here tonight."

Wall o' Meat grumbled. "Obviously that's not the case."

"But the Maytags are playing!"

I added my voice to the chorus of agreements.

"That's not my problem." Brick o' Meat gestured. "Time for you to go."

I leaned in and whispered: "Time to show me what you're made of!" and then pulled back.

"Yeah!" The band member that I'd whispered at pushed forward. "We're not going to take this from you, you know, it's a free country."

"Phil!" one of the other bouncers called from the door. "The crowd's getting kinda big, man. What should we do?"

"We'll play outside with the Maytags then!" the leader of the band cried, triumphantly. "We can do an acoustic concert too! We're just as good!"

"Brampton rules!" someone shouted in a burst of misplaced enthusiasm.

"Phil! Where are we going to put everyone?" demanded one of the other bouncers.

"Let's go," I whispered, giving nudges, and the six members of Straight Messina responded as I hoped.

"Yeah! Let's go! Let's do this!"

"Hey, can you get my guitar case, it's by your feet—"

"Someone's standing on my cape!"

"This is so cool! Like being on Much Unplugged!"

"That's the spirit, seize the moment," I urged in an undertone.

Phil the bouncer flung his hands up in defeat, waving

them towards the door. "Whatever. Whatever! You just need to get out of here, okay!" He turned to shout over his shoulder. "Get them out the door, Joe, god, what am I paying you for?" He turned his back long enough for me to squeeze by at the tail end of the band, and we emerged into safety and the cooler air.

In the moonlight, Straight Messina were all wearing KISS-esque makeup along with fake mullets and fedora hats and capes. I blinked in confusion while they stared up at me expectantly. The oldest looked barely old enough to shave. I'm not that old, am I?

"There's no room," one of them said plaintively to me.

Indeed there wasn't, and the free space on the sidewalk grew narrower by the moment. The Maytags were doing a... spirited... cover of Oasis' *Wonderwall*, in the style of... I'm not sure what. I felt very old and extremely non-hip. Peering around, I locked eyes by accident with Phil the Bouncer. He recognized me. And whatever gears he kept for thinking were turning. "Shit."

"What?"

"The other sidewalk is clear! Come on! Let's get you set up!"

"Don't you represent the Maytags?"

"I represent a lot of different people," I retorted. "And I want to see what you kids can do. So I'm going to stand in the middle of both bands and see who wins."

"...what?"

The bouncer pushed his way towards us, fury gathered in his face. "Come on!" I hustled. "You know, like a rock battle! Toronto's Blackout Battle of the Bands! Who will win! Who will lose! Exciting stuff! I can't wait!" With a combination of shoves and cajoling, I got Straight Messina across the street safely and directed them to set up as if I knew.

The lead singer stared, confused and hopeful and just a little dim. Dim and trusting. "Come on, kid, show me what you've got," I said, confident, then ducked around some people walking past. I flashed them a final thumbs up as they started singing, and then disappeared into the crowd.

What can I say about Straight Messina? Well, they were really, *really* bad. And loud! Whatever else those kids had going for them, they had the lungs of opera singers. Opera singers who did free-diving, and didn't let tone-deafness stand in the way of a good time.

The Maytags took this competition as a personal affront and sang louder.

There may not have been a Battle of the Bands *planned* for that night, but there certainly was one now, and the crowd was into it. Lighters sparked up and people cheered. There weren't many cars, but there were some in either direction, and as the audience spilled out onto the street, the traffic built up on either side, the frequent and intense honking adding to the cacophony and attracting more commotion from the neighbourhood. People leaned out their windows and left their stifling-hot apartments for a distraction from sitting in the dark.

If I wasn't so exhausted, it would have been great fun to watch.

The Maytags and Straight Messina seemed to find this crowd intoxicating, and by that I mean they threw themselves into their shitty music like cliff-jumpers, and the crowd clapped and cheered the sheer enthusiasm. Protected from the bouncers by the crush of people, I stayed to listen for a few minutes, appreciating my unmelodious handiwork. But this wasn't getting me home.

So I slipped back across the street, safely away from Lee's Palace, and rejoined the trudgers heading west.

14.
SHOVELLING HORSESHIT

It hadn't been even half a block before I noticed someone in a blue sedan slowly following me, peering out their window, craning to catch a better glimpse. The glimpses of face over my shoulder was annoyingly familiar, but the actions were too skeevy for anyone I would be friends with, and that meant... "Oh, you have got to be kidding me. Leave me alone, man. Come on." I picked up my pace, and the car honked at me.

Honked at me.

That was it. Fuming, I turned on my heel and marched up to the window. I expected to see an older, shaved head and a pin-striped suit, but instead it was someone about my age with dark hair and a bit of a beard. "Holy shit."

Mike grinned at me. "I thought it might be you, Mallory." His accent seemed stronger than I remembered from high school. "What are you doing out here?"

"Trying to get home," I told him, bending over to lean in through the window. "Nightmare of a day. But glad to see a familiar face. It's been a while."

East of us, the Maytags were winning the clash of rock bands; the lead singer remained audible blocks away even without amps. Shame he chose to scream obscene lyrics with them instead of anything productive. Like yodelling. Or shouting down a mine shaft. Really, I supported anything he chose to do with said lungs except shriek in the middle of the night out on Bloor Street. Still: gold star for effort.

That being said, he didn't clear the high note that he aimed for, and both Mike and I winced. Leaning over, he opened the passenger door. "Get in. I'll give you a lift."

I've never heard such sweetness. I tried to scoot into the proffered front seat but he held up a hand to pause me, while pushing clutter into the back.

"Sorry. I was not expecting a passenger. Where are you heading?"

"Islington. But any bit of the way would be great. Anything's better than walking." I closed the door, mentally crossing my fingers.

He hummed thoughtfully to himself, pulling out of the traffic to turn left on Euclid and then into a Green P parking lot. The lot was deserted and bleak without the overhead lamps.

I looked over at him with a silent question. Mike had never been a big talker; naturally quiet and thoughtful, but his thick Russian accent had led to some schoolyard teasing, causing him to chat even less. I'd worked with him on a few projects over the five years of high school, back in the days of OAC, including dramatic productions—he was a bit of a theatre nerd, helping out behind the scenes on everything that the cranky old drama teacher would let him, even hand-sewing at one point—and we became, not exactly friends, but we nodded at each other in the halls of Etobicoke Collegiate. You know how high school is.

He got out of the car, and I followed, still none the wiser as to why we were parked. "So, how have you been?" I asked, voice raised, while the Maytags and Straight Messina battled to a cheering crowd only a block away. "I haven't seen you in years. Been good?"

"Oh, yes, fine," Mike agreed, popping the trunk. "Can you do me a favour?"

"Sure?" He tossed a small plastic bag, knotted at the top, which I caught one-handed; it had the familiar lumps of empty Tim Horton's cups. "Want me to throw this out?"

"Am sorry, I live out of my car most days." He smiled at me as he hustled an armload of long tools from the back seat—that's what must have been poking up—and dumped them into the trunk.

I wandered to the dumpsters on the edge of the parking lot. Tripping over an unseen pothole, my ankle turned on itself and I stumbled. Thankfully I didn't fall, but my high heel developed an unnerving and unsecured wobble. "Oh, of course." I dunked the bag of road-trip empties into the trash with vengeance.

Mike, meanwhile, was using his foot to push something down in the trunk when I came back. His face was illuminated by sickly yellow light from inside the car. He glanced up as I approached and then slammed the trunk down.

"Need any help?"

"No, no, it's fine." He hurried around the car to open the door for me. "Here."

"Thank you." I was too tired to do anything but accept graciously and I made myself comfortable in the front seat. That being said, best mention Dylan as soon as I 'naturally' could, before Mike got any ideas. "Live out of your car, eh?"

He agreed, starting the engine. "I help my uncles with their business, so I spend a lot of time running errands."

"Landscaping?" I asked, as we started on our journey, heading south on Euclid to avoid the crowd.

He blinked, then nodded. "Yes, something like that. How did you know?"

"The shovels."

"Oh, yes, the shovels." He laughed. "Thing is, I am running an errand for my uncle now, but then I promise I will drive you home."

Shit. "I really don't want this to be a bother. I mean—"

"It's not bother," he assured me. "Really. I drive all the time. Company is nice. You can tell me how you have been. It's been many years."

I swallowed, feeling a red flag unfurl in my mind. It had been a day of shitty people doing shitty things, but I was being cynical. I mean, I'd seen nice people doing nice things too. Right? "Well, you know, I mean, yeah. I guess I don't know where to start. I work in sales—"

"Really? Me too," he said, cheerfully.

"I thought you worked in landscaping?"

"That too. Sales *in* landscaping. But sometimes I help with other things. It's a... family business, you know, so we all have to help where we can."

"Sure," I agreed. "Of course. I always figured you'd go into the theatre."

We were heading east now on Harbord, the small houses dark and quiet. We startled a cyclist with our high beams—that takes nerve, to cycle with no streetlights—but other than that, there was no other traffic. Mike laughed. "Theatre? Why would you think that?"

"Well, you always helped out in drama class."

"Oh. Ha ha ha. Yes. But drama was fun and easy. That's all. Wasn't that why you were there?"

"I guess so. I wanted to take an art class but drawing was full, so I figured I could paint backdrops or something."

"My parents wanted me to become a doctor, so I took all those math and biology classes, but they were so boring. I told them, here in Canada you must take drama classes too, everyone must, is standard, and they believed me." He smiled, fondly remembering. We turned north on Spadina. He seemed just as quietly friendly as I remembered from school. A pleasant enough partner in class but too quiet, and we never hung out afterwards.

The few times I'd tried asking him about himself he'd gotten a panicked expression on his face and clammed up tighter than usual. In my myopic teenager way I'd assumed it was because he was, like, totally weird or something, so I stopped asking. I'd spent most of my social time in high school learning how not to stand out and glide through the classes until I could make my escape.

But Mike didn't seem any different from what I remembered. Older, obviously, and he'd filled out in the way that weedy teenage boys often did later in life, but he still had his open face and a pleasant manner, and didn't say any more than he needed to. He watched me out of the corner of his eye. "You want music on? Or air-conditioning?"

"I'm fine, thanks."

He nodded. "One small errand, then I take you home. You are married?"

"No, but I live with my boyfriend, Dylan." This was safer, firmer ground.

"Dylan?" He pried apart the syllables. "He is Irish? Or Canadian."

"Well, his mother was originally from Ireland but she lived her most of her life here. His father is from Peru."

"Ah."

"How about you? Married?"

"Yes, three years now. We have a baby girl. Here, in dashboard, there is a picture, you can see."

And so the car ride unfolded, and I relaxed.

It was a luxury to be travelling at a decent pace. The car was comfortable, there was sweet blessed air-conditioning, and Mike didn't seem to notice that I was a sweaty mess. Or maybe he did but he didn't say anything.

I told him the Coles Notes version of my day, leaving out the weirdness at Honest Ed's, and that strange businessman I kept running into. He laughed really hard at the students in the car and the fight with the aunt and uncle and it brought me back to our high school days where I could have him laughing over almost anything; he often belly-laughed over turns of phrase I found only mildly amusing, but it did make for fun study sessions.

Hearing him talk about his own life made me happy for him; he'd shed his former awkwardness. Transplanted from his home as a teenager had taken some of the life out of him, but he now was settled and, as he called it, "blooming". And that was great. But whenever I asked him about his family's business he went a bit cagey.

"It's very boring work."

"All work is boring. That's why it's work. Otherwise it would be fun."

This caused him to laugh so hard he slapped the steering wheel, repeating it to himself under his breath and shaking his head. (Sometimes we change from when we were teenagers, and sometimes we don't.) "I like that."

"It's yours. Feel free to use it whenever." I made an expansive hand gesture of freedom, very Vanna White, but doing so moved the fabric of my jacket around and gave me a snootful of my own stink. I winced. "Do you mind if we turn down the AC and open the windows instead?"

He frowned, then nodded, already reaching for the dial. I wound my window a couple of inches, three or four turns of the handle. "That's much better." The air blowing in was sweet with perfume; the house we passed had a fence covered in orange flowers, all still open. "Those smell good."

Mike glanced out my window, then nodded. "Ah. Honeysuckle."

"Is that what honeysuckle looks like? Huh."

He made a face, and the silence grew awkward. I didn't know what to say, but finally, he said, quietly: "The smell. It is a problem."

I froze, appalled at myself. Should I apologize? Laugh it off? Pretend I wasn't as rank as a mule?

He frowned, embarrassed.

"I'm really sorry," I said in a tiny voice.

"It's not your fault!" He seemed surprised.

"Well, no, I mean, yes, but it's been a long day. I put on deodorant on this morning," I added, shrinking down in my seat.

His rather expansive eyebrows gathered together to confer and then he relaxed, bursting out into loud laughter. "You think you are the smell!" All I could do was stare. Of course I smelled, what else was he talking about?

I took some experimental sniffs. I hadn't noticed earlier because my own stink had bothered me more, being closer to my nose. But there was a different, unsettling smell in the car, an earthy aroma with a vaguely metallic undertone. I peeked behind us, but it was too dark to see beyond there being a dark bundle on the back seat against the beige velour. "What does your family do again?" I asked, conversationally. "I know you told me, but honestly I am so tired I can't remember what my own name is."

Mike glanced back at me out of the corner of his eye. "You can smell it," he said. It wasn't a question.

I tried to shrug but my nose wrinkled instead, involuntarily.

"We do all sorts of things," he said, the lightness gone from his voice. He was turning into one of the suburbs off Bathurst. We'd come pretty far north; I hadn't been paying too much attention, but I guessed we were just south of Wilson. "I do, how you say, the weird jobs."

"The weird... jobs."

"I forget what it is called in English. I usually speak Russian more now."

I thought for a moment. "Do you mean 'odd jobs'?"

He brightened. "Yes! I do the odd jobs. That is why I am running errand now, at night."

Running errands at night. Sure, that made sense. The earthy smell tugged at my senses, urging me to recall what it reminded me of. Besides dirt, I mean.

"Sometimes, it is unavoidable," Mike continued. "The smell. This one, it is a bit odd, but she is a good paying client, and she asks us a favour and we do the favour, you know?"

"Sure," I agreed. Then: "What *is* that smell?" But even

as I spoke, I knew.

"It is..." he paused, focusing on parking, pulling up to the side of the street outside a dark house surrounded by other large, dark houses. If it hadn't smelled like what I was worried it smelled like, the air would have given off the odour of new money. He sighed, turning off the car. "Is dead cat."

I stared at him. "Dead cat."

He gave an expansive shrug. "She is old, maybe a little crazy, who can say? But when she moves, the dead cat has to come with her. To go in the new backyard."

"You are trying to tell me that there is a decomposing cat in your back seat."

"Yes." Straight face, his hands in his lap, torso twisted in the driver's seat to face me full on. I recognized that openness; that was the openness of someone trying not to look like their pants were on fire.

I was in the middle of nowhere with someone lying to me about having a dead cat in the back seat and shovels in the trunk who was running errands in the middle of the night for his Russian family.

Oh god.

"That's very gross," I admitted, adopting the I'm-not-a-con-artist pose myself. I was in a car with a Russian mobster. "The dead cat, I mean."

"It is. Very gross. Alek had to dig it up, now it is in a box, and I wrapped the box in the plastic, uh, the plastic tarp." He hooked a thumb behind him to indicate the back seat, then put his hands back in his lap. "I am very sorry."

"There's a dead cat in the back seat," I repeated, nodding to myself. Trying to give the impression that I was saying, 'sure why not' when in reality my mind raced around waving its arms like a demented muppet.

"Why didn't... Alek drive it?"

"Oh, I had to clean the car tomorrow anyway," he said, easily, as if this was the simplest thing in the world. "Because of the other dirt."

"The other dirt."

"Yes. Not enough space in the trunk before so the buckets were in the front seat. With the shovels." He's got such a kind face, Mike; like an overgrown boy scout. And he was being completely honest with me, obviously except for the teeny detail that this was all a load of horseshit and I was sitting in a car in god-knows-where *North York* with a Russian mob errand boy.

Movement outside the car. Mike glanced out and then wound down his window, speaking in Russian. A man leaned over, resting his forearm on the door frame, peering in at me. "Hello."

"Hi," I said. Stay calm, Mallory. Don't look like you realize. Just play it cool.

"This is Roman, my cousin," Mike said. Roman gave a tired wave, wearing a suit and gold jewelry and looking about as much like a landscaper as I do. They conversed in Russian; Roman nodded, gave Mike a slap on the shoulder, and departed.

Mike spread his hands, apologetic. "This won't take long. I have to take the cat, and something from the trunk, and talk for a bit with my cousins, and then I will take you home. I promise."

I forced myself to smile. "Sure." The moment he was gone I was going to flee. That much was sure.

Mike got out to deal with the lump in the back seat. The overhead light came on and the lump looked more like a box, or a tote, draped in a tarp. He picked it up under one arm—who would *do* that—before disappearing between the houses into someone's backyard.

I opened my door and slid silently out.

"Hello," someone said behind me, and I screamed and leapt in the air, whirling around with my fists up. What that would accomplish, I don't know, but sometimes fists just want to up, it's how fists think sometimes.

A younger-looking version of Roman—thinner, more hair to style with too much gel, not dressed in a suit but a hoodie over jeans—leaned against the trunk. He must have come out with Roman and I didn't notice. It's dark out!

He laughed, sounding an awful lot like Mike. "Sorry to scare you." He didn't have any accent at all. "You're Mike's friend?"

"That's me," I replied, lowering my hands, tugging my jacket smooth, trying to laugh it off. "You startled me."

The kid smiled, giving me elevator eyes—ugh—and then looked around at the eerily silent and blacked-out neighbourhood. "Bad day, huh."

"Yeah, a super nightmare," I replied, easily, leaning against the car myself. No way I could outrun anyone in my heels if it came to that. Probably better to wait for a moment to slip away. "Transit down, buses are running out of gas, streetcars left in the middle of the streets, all that."

"Yeah," the kid replied, nodding. "The geezers are all talking about how it reminds them of the old days, but give them anything to talk about at all and it'll remind them of the old days."

"Ha ha, yeah, I bet. Old guys, right?" I awkwardly crossed my arms and tried to think casual thoughts. "So how do you know Mike?"

The kid didn't answer because someone called out in Russian at him. It was Mike himself, coming back to the car, dusting off his hands. "Alek, there you are. Are you helping or are you talking?"

"I can do both," Alek replied sullenly. "That horrible thing out back?"

Mike noticed me standing, giving a quizzical tilt of his head.

"It's cooler out here," I said. "And, the smell—"

He nodded, understanding. "Oh, of course. Again, I'm sorry about that."

"Not your fault," I replied easily. "Dead cats. New yard. Happens to everyone eventually." My former study partner seemed a bit confused and Alek graced me with a grin that I didn't like.

"Mike," he said, eyes still on me, "it's a bit creepy out here. Maybe your friend should come in with us, have some tea or something while we wait for Uncle Lev."

"Oh, I'm fine." But Mike thought I was protesting politely because he immediately made it clear that I should follow him. "Really, I'm fine."

"No, no, come, have some tea."

"We insist," Alek added, with the shit-eating-est grin I have ever seen on a person. Then to Mike he said: "I'll bring the... stuff from the trunk."

I flashed a look between them. "Stuff". The way he said it and I *knew*. I knew exactly what he was thinking. Alek added something in Russian, and Mike's face clouded, then cleared. I have no idea what that meant but I didn't like it.

"Yes," he said, carefully. "Come have tea with us. I insist."

Swallowing, I followed behind him, Alek bringing up the rear, carrying a huge tote.

15.
CATCHING UP

Deep breaths, Mallory, act calm. Maybe you can sneak away to the bathroom or something. The house was a two-storey detached, the kind with a double-garage that faced the street; beige brickwork and aluminium siding; a little paved pathway to the backyard behind a tall wooden fence. I could have been anywhere in southern Ontario. I had to step carefully over the grass, my heels wanted to sink in the soft earth. So well-watered, even with the dry summer we'd been having. Wasn't there a water advisory on?

Mike led us to a small door in the side of the garage. Light glowed around its edges. Stepping in, I found it graced by a few small camping lanterns and an actual glass kerosene antique pioneer contraption. Less a garage than a workshop, with a small kitchenette and a table and chairs.

The men waiting inside all stood. All older, comfortably jowled, scowling, with more jewellery than I'd consider tasteful, shiny watches. Mike clapped a hand down on my shoulder and I flinched a little, not gonna lie. He spoke to them in Russian and they all stared at me. I caught my name several times, as well as *Etobicoke*.

They seemed to relax and one of them gestured towards the kitchenette where a hot plate was plugged into one of those portable generators that takes a car battery. "I just made tea. You want some?"

"I'm fine," I squeaked.

Alek pushed past us, dumping the tote on the ground, dusting off his hands. "Here it is. All of it."

"You sure?" One of the middle-aged men opened the lid, and pulled out a clear packet, about the size of a coffee bag, but filled with white crystals. He threw it on the table and they all peered at it, nodding approvingly at Mike and Alek.

I am really glad I managed to find a toilet at Lee's Palace because this is the part where I would have peed myself.

Still with Mike's hand on my shoulder, I tried to slide a bit out of the way but he kept a grip and I couldn't. "Now, we wait."

"Wait?" My voice made a comical impression of myself on helium. I swallowed. "For who?"

"Where is Roman?" one of the men asked, his voice so heavily accented it sounded like an extra from *Hunt For Red October*. Like a Hollywood version of a Russian.

"He's just checking on something," Alek said, watching for my reaction.

"Maybe I should wait outside or back by the car, let you guys do your business, I don't want to be in the way." I was babbling and the grip on my shoulder tightened. Just a bit. Just a squeeze telling me I wasn't going anywhere.

"Is that... cat... taken care of?" the man asked Alek.

"I don't know, that's Mike's job."

"I'm asking you, you do it."

"But—!" Alek switched to Russian, arguing, and yet everyone's eyes stayed on me.

"Just take care of it," the man said, sagging his bulk into a fold-away card table chair. He crossed meaty arms over his chest, regarding me with a scowl that seemed a permanent feature of his face. Alek stomped out of the garage, muttering.

"Shouldn't be long." Mike gave me a pat as he finally moved his hand away.

I tried to look anywhere but at the faces of the men surrounding me, or the table with the packet of crystalline powder, or the giant green tote *filled with drugs*. I ended up peering at the unfinished walls of the workshop, studying the insulation. In the low, flickering lights of the lanterns, it didn't fluff like cotton candy, but instead moved with ominous curls and grasping outreaches, like fingers. Something moved. Was that a mouse?

Suddenly the garage door swung open and lights blazed, right into my eyes, blinding. I screamed and recoiled, throwing my hands up over my face; the men leapt from their chairs, cursing in at least two different languages.

"Freeze! Police!"

I shoved myself backwards behind Mike and wedged myself down behind a plastic shelving unit, hands over my head.

The cursing devolved into heavy braying laughter, and I opened one eye cautiously into the beam of a flashlight, then it tilted up and away to reveal Alek, back with his shit-eating grin, and Roman.

They were all laughing at me, including Mike, who held out a hand to help me up. I blinked watering eyes, bewildered. "I told you, we do landscaping," he guffawed. "But you don't believe me, huh?"

One of the heavyset uncles in the chairs laughed so hard he started coughing, wiping tears away.

"Seriously." Alek clicked his flashlight off. "How gullible *are* you?"

I swallowed, relieved and embarrassed and foolish all at the same time. "I—" I held out my hands helplessly. "You wouldn't believe the day I've had if I told you."

"Mobsters," Roman sniffed, making himself a cup of tea. "I wish. The money would be better."

"...The dead cat?" I asked Mike.

"Is dead cat. I'm not lying. Crazy old woman wants her dead cat in her new backyard. She pays extra, so what do we care?" He leaned against the shelving, grinning at me, arms crossed. "Your face. You think we really are mobsters."

"Then what's that?" I pointed at the tote.

One of the older men picked the packet up and then tossed it back in the tote. "Fertilizer, mostly. Some, how do you say it, Alek?"

"Pesticide."

"Yes, for the weeds."

"Fertilizer and pesticides," I repeated. "Because you do landscaping."

"Because we do landscaping." Mike grinned.

"And you're doing this at midnight because...?"

"Because I was out all day trying to make sales," Roman said, slurping his tea. "It is very weird hours. And then this power out—"

"Yeah." I nodded, then rubbed the bridge of my nose. "Landscaping."

Mike laughed again and clapped me on the back so hard that I staggered. "Come. I give you a ride home."

"No! Stay for food," one of the men protested, jovially. "We have leftovers! Propane barbeque. You must eat. Come, come."

I weakened, tempted by the idea of barbeque, but Mike already had his hand on the door handle, and I was so tired. "Thank you, but no."

He waved me away, no hard feelings. They were all still grinning at me, shaking their heads, pleased with their joke. I'd made their day.

I leaned against the side of the car, arms resting on the roof. "Oh my god, I can't believe that just happened."

Mike's grin came back. "You looked so funny."

"You had me fooled."

"You really think I am criminal?"

"No! I mean, no, not you. But I don't know your family, and then you started in with the dead cat thing, and running errands in the middle of the night, and I don't know, man, I just... the things I've seen today, this isn't even the weirdest." I ran a hand over my hair. "I just can't wait to get home."

"Then let's get you home," Mike agreed, that openness back on his face. It was the expression of a decent person and I felt even more foolish for having fallen for the stereotypes in the first place.

I had my hand on the door handle. I remember closing my fingers around it, so close to going home. But then there was a sudden loud squeal of tires and a car sped around the corner of the winding, suburban street. The windows were open, someone shouted at us, and then I got hit with something. I screamed and ducked behind the car, checking myself for a wound, but it was a crumpled up Tim Horton's Iced Capp container that they'd chucked at me. "What the fuck!"

Mike shouted at the car that had overshot us and was now braking, red tail-lights like animal eyes in the dark. Doors opened. Alek and Roman came running when they heard my scream and joined Mike in the street.

"I thought you said you weren't mobsters!"

"We aren't," Mike protested.

"What the fuck." Roman growled. "Who the fuck is this? What are they doing shouting at us?"

There were four men, and they were advancing. Alek swung his flashlight at their faces, and I realized with sickening horror who it was: the businessman, the one in the pinstripe suit. I didn't know the others, but I knew him.

"They don't want you." Panic spread up and around me like strangling vines. "They're here for me!"

One of the men threw something else—more garbage—and it hit Alek. He threw down the flashlight and charged at them like only a stupid young man can do, breaking out of Roman's grip.

"Stay here," Mike told me, already running after his cousin. The older men streamed out of the garage, and shouting in Russian filled the lane.

I remained crouched by the car. This was all my fault. Somehow, for some reason, I'd brought the pinstripe suit man and now there was a fight going on.

Maybe I should have stayed and tried to explain. Next time this happens, I'll remember to do that, to stand up and be the bigger person and wade in and talk it all out. But that's not what I did.

Instead I ran, the sound of my heels on the asphalt lost in the commotion.

16.
DOWN AT HEEL

I leaned against a fence in a rabbit warren of suburban houses somewhere in North-Fucking-York with honest-to-Ed's goons behind me. I mean, I have to assume goonery. How that pin-stripe-suited motherfucker kept finding me, I don't know.

What had Chantuelle called it? An 'embargo'? It had sounded ridiculous under cover of afternoon, but anything at all seemed more likely in the middle of the night.

I peered around for signposts, street signs, hoping to recognize at least something. But I appeared to be at the corner of butt-fuck and nowhere. There wasn't even the glow of the core against the southern sky to guide me.

"Toronto slopes south" had been parroted at me ever since my first visit, and maybe it does when you're on Yonge Street, but it certainly doesn't slope consistently *everywhere* and whole neighbourhoods were built where it was flat. Like here. Flat as a pancake. The CN tower wasn't visible. The lake wasn't visible. Just stupid post-war bungalows and trees and parked cars, all featureless silhouettes under the starlight.

So I literally picked a direction at random to walk. Eventually, goes the reasoning, I would hit a larger street, and from there figure out where the hell I was. And so I stepped confidently off the curb.

And my heel fucking snapped off.

The instability pitched me forward; I yanked myself backward in an attempt to stay upright; I over-yanked; I fell flat on my ass. And it hurt.

I sat there, legs out on the street, smarting ass on the curb, trying to catch my breath and keep from bursting into tears, rubbing my chilly arms. Eventually the sniffling passed and my resolve came back. Nothing to do but pick myself up and keep going, unless I wanted to sleep on the sidewalk. No guarantee power would be on in the morning, either.

So I pulled myself up, dusting the grit of the road off my skirt and wiping my face. Every time I stretched, my ripped sleeve gaped at me. I bent down and picked up the chunk of heel off the street; maybe I could glue the shoes back together.

I took a wobbling step in my broken shoes. It was like limping. I had to stand on my tip-toes, all the pressure on my blisters and they burned in protestation, bringing more tears to my eyes. I took a few more tentative steps before there came a tearing sensation on my toes and unpleasant wetness. I sat back on the curb, taking off my pumps to survey the damage. Yep. All my blisters had ripped open and were now bleeding.

"That's super." I no longer cared if anyone heard me talking to myself. "That's just fucking fantastic. I will probably die of blood poisoning after this. I hope Dylan fucking learns the day I've had at my fucking funeral." I wiggled my toes. It hurt. But worse than the pain of

my feet—well, maybe not worse but still pretty bad—
was the vision of Dylan and Camila on my patio, eating
my meal, drinking *my* beer, enjoying *them*selves
together.

*Except, let's be honest, it's the middle of the night. That
meal is long gone. Dylan's probably asleep. Hopefully by
himself.*

The mental image gutted me more than the bloody
blisters or bruised butt and I scrunched up my face to
keep from bursting into tears. Camila wasn't going to
win that easily. I was going to get home, I was going to
sleep for two days and eat a whole pizza and have a
long hot bath—not entirely sure what order, although
likely food first—and then I was going to march—
stride—hobble—across the hall and tell that bitch
exactly what I thought of her and her stupid fluttering
eyelashes and her always coming over to reinforce that
she could speak Spanish to my boyfriend and I could
not.

I took a few deep breaths, the kind where you inhale
smoothly but they come out as shuddering, jagged
exhales, one step from ugly crying. My stomach
cramped, not even rumbling any more. One more pain
in the pile.

Suddenly from my left was a crunch of feet on the
asphalt, and the noise jerked me out of my misery with
a booster shot of alarm. But it wasn't any mobsters or
identical businessmen in matching suits or even
someone who might have been a schnauzer once upon
a time.

It was a lanky teenager, and they didn't notice me.
They had headphones on as they wheeled out the
garbage bin. No one else on the street had bothered;
from the sulky expression on the teenager's face I had
a notion they were being told to do their chores

regardless of circumstances. They set up the bin, threw a pizza box on top, and walked away, head bobbing to the music.

The pizza box slid off the top, landing on a corner, the lid flipping open. Something poked out.

My stomach recoiled and rumbled at the same time.

My mouth watered and my brain protested.

Feeling remote-controlled, I got up. *I'm just going to see what's in there.*

This is revolting.

I'm just going to see if there's an untouched slice left. That would be okay, right? An untouched slice?

This is a new low point in the history of low points, Mallory.

But I kept walking, limping with one heel on and the other in my hand. I didn't even think about my toes. Hating myself but still crouching, I opened up the pizza box. There were a few crusts left. Not a whole slice; just crusts. I poked one; not stale. Maybe from earlier in the day, before the blackout.

Don't.

How hungry was I, really?

I picked up one of the crusts.

How hungry *was* I?

A weird growling sound answered, but it wasn't my stomach. I glanced over my shoulder, startled to find a fat raccoon, maybe a yard from me, under the hedge. It was growling at me, like a cat. Do raccoons do that? Maybe *it* had once been a schnauzer.

I swallowed, still holding on to one of the pizza crusts.

The raccoon didn't back down.

"This is mine." I hissed back at it, and it bared its teeth. "Go get your own." But then came a rustle. Eyes shining in the starlight. Many eyes. It wasn't one raccoon, but a mother with a bunch of mostly-growns, and they were all looking at me.

When I was a teen, we had a neighbour whose cat scattered cat food all over her kitchen every night after she went to bed. She couldn't figure out how the cat did it because the food was in the cupboard and her pet was not the brightest kitten in the litter box. Since I babysat her kids sometimes, I volunteered to help her figure the problem out and we'd hung out with her one night, sitting on the floor with the lights off, to watch how her dumbass cat managed this feat.

After the sun went down, there was rustling outside. As we watched, a little clawed hand appeared, managing to slide between the door jamb and the rickety wooden-framed screen door. It slid up under the hook and eye latch, and neatly flipped it open.

Then the raccoon let itself in. It waddled to the bottom cupboard in the kitchen where the lady kept her cat food, opening the door, pulling the bag out and spilling it across the linoleum, stuffing its face in the process.

Wordlessly and with wide eyes, she'd gotten a broom and given the raccoon a careful poke. Not hard; a nudge. It looked over its shoulder at us with an affronted expression of "Do you *mind*? I am trying to *eat*" before resuming its chow.

She nudged it again while I grabbed the mop. Together we'd fought the raccoon out the door while it growled and swiped at us. It had made a noise an awful lot like the noise this one made at me. And I did not have a broom or a solid door to close, and my feet were bleeding.

I put down the crust of pizza and closed the box.

Mama lunged and I shrieked and bounced to my feet, the pain making my vision sparkle.

I threw my broken shoe.

The pump bounced off one of the younger raccoons; it didn't so much as yelp, merely staggering momentarily before proceeding to the feast. Mama chattered at me in the peeved manner that raccoons have that sounds like a cocktail party from two floors away.

They watched me retreat, their eyes glittering.

I might have been hungry, but I wasn't 'fight a pack of Toronto raccoons for pizza crusts' hungry.

Maybe now. Maybe now was the time.

I took off my remaining shoe and tucked it under my arm, walking down the middle of the street on the pads of my heels, my toes lifted up like my nails were drying. It was slow but it hurt less.

I walked until I came to a four-way stop, the houses all shuttered around me. And there, in the moonlight, out of the shadow of the leafy trees lining the streets, I took out the cell phone from my pocket.

I couldn't ask him to call me a cab since I didn't know where I was. He couldn't pick me up; we don't have a car. He was probably asleep. He'd already given up on me coming home any time soon, probably thinking I was crashing at Aggie's or something like that.

I held the little Nokia out into the moonlight so that I could see its tiny blank screen, like a sleeping face, a baby's, all innocent. I'd been manhandled by TTC officers; incorporeal; nearly trapped in an unreal Honest Ed's; beholden to who knows who—and I hadn't yet called in case some 'bigger emergency' happened. But I was shoeless and desperate enough to eat garbage, if not yet fight off overgrown vermin for the privilege of doing so.

Dylan couldn't help me. But at least he could tell me

that it would all be okay.

Taking a deep breath, I pressed power.

The screen booted up; still the one bar left. Hard to tell. I had to both bring it to my face to see but also tilt it to get the maximum out of the moonlight. But it looked like there were words—

—my hands shook.

Where it usually said ROGERS it said NO SIGNAL.

I shivered like I was freezing, although the August night was anything but. I clutched at the little Nokia like it was a rope and I was drowning, my knuckles bloodless. NO SIGNAL. I typed in Dylan's number anyway and pressed the call button, but no dial tone answered me. Not even a beep.

I pulled the phone away from my ear and stared at NO SIGNAL for an eternity until the battery drained. The screen flashed and the phone powered down.

All this wandering, saving the battery. Holding off on calling Dylan when I had the chance, because I had the cell phone—and the whole time, there was no signal. Belatedly, stupidly, cursedly, I realized that there hadn't been since the blackout started; the cell towers would all be down. They weren't like landlines, that kept working without power. The technology was so new to me that I didn't think it through.

I'd been keeping the cell phone back, keeping it as my emergency life-saving and this whole time there'd been no use. It wouldn't have worked. A useless hunk of company plastic, and I couldn't even trade it for streetmeat because it wasn't mine to trade.

I sank to the asphalt, legs curled under me, no idea where I was or what time it was or when power would come back to the world. "I'm so sorry," I said, quietly, my voice thick and my eyes burning. "I'm sorry for whatever I did. Whatever caused the embargo. I just want to go home, please. If anyone is listening."

But the only answer was the rustle of the breeze in the tree tops along the sleeping suburban street.

The good thing about being so tired that you can barely breathe is that it turns everything into a sort of fog. A fog of exhaustion and numbness. The pain from my toes receded to a part of my brain that certainly remained aware of it, but didn't let it stop me walking. Because those were my choices; continue walking or sleep on the sidewalk.

I suppose one of the houses around me held a nice, kind, loving person who practised the sort of hospitality that sagas and religions are born from, the kind who would not only give me bandaids and a meal but maybe also a guest bed and a long shower. (Or at least a couch and a sandwich.) But there was no way to tell which of these sleeping bungalows had such a respectable, decent person, and which ones held assholes with shotguns.

That's where I felt like my night was headed: assholes with shotguns.

Eventually I walked larger streets that funnelled me to the park. No, not a park, a square; it was paved. From its opposite corner I could hear traffic. Finally an artery to gain my bearings. All I wanted at this point was to trudge in the right direction.

First I had to weave through the dark buildings, past a plaza with a fountain. People were still out, even though it was clearly the middle of the night. Or was it the middle of the night? I actually had no idea. But yes, there were people, little knots of families escaping their darkened, breathless homes.

A breeze wove through in the square, and people had

brought tiny battery-powered radios and lanterns, spreading blankets to enjoy the rare sight of stars and relief from the stifling humidity. I supposed that if I lived in an apartment building with no cross-breeze I might well have gone outside to sleep too. Someone plucked at a guitar, a real one, not a banjo. Kids splashed in the fountain.

My head spun. I walked across strips of dewy grass, the cold softness a mercy to my feet. Nearby under the trees were picnic tables. A glow of light. A family setting up a picnic, and I stopped, watching them with longing. The mother brought out sandwiches from a cooler and the adolescents were so bored it was palpable.

The dad noticed me watching them and I tensed, ready to make my apologies and back away before he took offence. But he wasn't glaring. The woman and the kids saw me, and she waved me over, even after I hesitated.

I felt lumpen, like someone trapped in a metal suit. I could barely bend, speak, nod when they asked me questions. Everything about me creaked slow and stupid and I didn't want to cry in front of these nice strangers, they were clean and pleasant and obviously lived nearby and had never once considered fighting a raccoon off for pizza crusts.

They were making coffee, did I want some?

Don't cry, Mallory, don't cry.

They had sandwiches, would I like one?

Just hold it together a little longer.

And then the mom smiled at me, said I looked like I'd had quite the day.

And then she said, just start at the beginning.

PART TWO

Mallory chewed and swallowed as a profound silence settled over the picnic table. Shelly offered her a plastic tumbler of water, which she accepted, all without a sound. The water was so refreshing that it tasted sweet; although that might have been residual peanut butter. She couldn't believe how worn she felt.

"That's some story, hun," Shelly said, finally, her arm around her boy, watching the storyteller solemnly with lantern flickers dancing in his widened eyes. "Could have been maybe a bit more... kid-friendly?"

"Sorry." Mallory winced. "I guess I just got into it."

"It's not like we haven't heard the word 'fuck' before." The girl, Dawn, rested her head in her hand, elbow on the rough surface of the picnic table, so bored—or sleepy—that her eyes were at half-mast even while she spoke. "I mean. Come on, Mom."

"Still." Shelly hugged her son. "What did you think of the story, Dee?"

"What about Dylan?" the boy whispered, blinking back emotion under his thick black lashes. "You never called him."

"No, I didn't," Mallory agreed, the cell phone pressing against her ribs as both an accusation and a disappointment. "But he'll understand." This last was under her breath. A vision of Camila leaning against the door frame, talking in Spanish, ignoring Mallory completely while she did so—came to mind so potently that tears sprang to her eyes.

"Okay!" Daniel Gabriel clapped his hands together brightly. "I think it's time for this old geezer to stretch his legs. Who wants to walk around the block with me?"

Teenage groans answered, while Shelly shook her head, curls bouncing over her shoulders. "You go. Take Mallory."

"Oh, Mallory's done enough walking for a lifetime," she answered, with a sad laugh. "Mallory's happy to stay sitting."

"Mallory should listen to a good idea when she hears one," Daniel Gabriel answered with a wink, getting to his feet. Standing, he was head and shoulders out of the light of the tiny Coleman lantern, but Mallory could still see his eyes glinting. "Come on. Walk with me."

The moon sat high overhead, back to its regular aspirin size, white and full and unimpeded by clouds, dusted with starlight. Crickets sang and chirped around them. Bushes in front yards rustled; branches creaked with the shift of a breeze. Somewhere, an owl hooted softly.

"I didn't even know we had owls in the city," Mallory said, feeling the sidewalk under her toes in a way she remembered from being a kid. "I suppose we must." She patted a lamppost as they passed, missing both its sodium glow and background hiss. So many noises that she'd never realized were there were gone. In the distance a car drove by, its headlights obscenely bright, the crunch of its tires on the asphalt like thunder.

"You get used to a way of thinking about the world," Daniel Gabriel said, his hands in his hoodie pockets. "Takes a special kind of day to make you realize how different things can be. No one gets a day like that very often. Some never get one at all."

Mallory wanted to snort cynically, mention how nothing would change, that humans didn't work like that, but she didn't. In the dark, such notions were worth considering.

Daniel Gabriel stopped. They'd come to the far end of the square, through tall buildings looming in the darkness, cut out of shadow against the stars like a cliff. Before them lay a cemetery, headstones and memorials brighter than they should have been in the moonlight. He gestured at Mallory's pocket. "I think you have something meant for me."

Confused, she shook her head, but then—because she couldn't think of a reason not to—she searched her tiny jacket pockets. In one lay her dead Nokia; in the other a thin rolled joint and a lighter. She held them out, waiting for him to choose.

He smiled, lighting the joint up with a well-practised flick, and taking a drag. His breath seemed to glitter in the night, as if he breathed the stars out. "You fucked up. You realize that, right?" He held the joint out, still smiling, showing no malice or sarcasm, only bemusement and sympathy. "I told you to be careful of contracts you didn't realize you were breaking."

Her own drag didn't taste as vegetative as she expected. More floral; delicately tinged with something else. Fruit of some kind. She exhaled out her nose, half-expecting stars too, but no, only dope smoke. She passed the joint back. "It was you at the party."

Daniel Gabriel nodded. "You asked for help. So I helped you."

"I don't remember asking."

"Maybe not exactly, but you said you were tired and hungry, and you sounded sad. I am a sucker for sad sacks." He blew out another breath, sighing, eyes half-closed. "And you helped my uncle, which means he owes me."

"I don't see how that works."

"Doesn't matter if you see how it works or not. Connections and contracts. Social structures, rules, conventions, communication. Also thieves and trickery, but that's neither here nor there right now." He leaned against a granite memorial, watching a black silhouette land in a nearby tree. The crow cawed once before alighting.

"Social contracts," Mallory repeated, sleepy. Her body maintained that weight of exhaustion. But something deep down in the bottom of her mind stirred, as if it had slept too long already. "Rules and communi—oh fuck."

"Told you." He held the joint out.

"That's what this has been about? This whole time? Skipping the fucking turnstile? I'd already paid to get in! I was going back to get my wallet!" Her drag caught against her lungs and she spluttered.

"That's not the point," he chided, "and you know it."

"I don't know what else I could've done."

"Then think harder."

She crossed her arms, jamming her hands into her armpits, and rested against a headstone, the name meaningless, the letters carved so deeply they never ended. The awoken part of her mind moved around, stretching, drawing open curtains. Normally weed made her a bit drowsy and goofy, with potential of munchies, but this wasn't like any joint she'd had before. A cream-soda taste lingered on her tongue and her nose. "I didn't have a metropass. I'd lost my wallet." She explained slowly, working through the steps. "The power was out. People were losing their minds. It was a special set of circumstances. Squints should have known that."

"How," Daniel Gabriel asked, the word hanging in the void, suspended and immortal until it dissipated, blown into nothing by his release of smoke, "would he have known that?"

He handed the joint out to her.

She wasn't sure if she wanted any more. But she took it anyway, considering the glowing ember at its tip. "You're saying I should have asked him? Asked him to let me in?"

Daniel Gabriel shrugged. "He's not a bad guy."

"Seems to have some issues."

"...well, yes." He sighed and rubbed the bridge of his nose. "Not real bright. Not a big fan of downtowners."

"I did get that impression."

"Shouldn't have grabbed you."

"No, he should not have."

Daniel Gabriel gave a nod of agreement. "I hereby apologize on his behalf. But—and this is the important part—if you'd asked for his help, you might have received it."

She licked her dry lips, considering, and then took one last small puff before handing it back. He stubbed it out on the memorial, flicking the end away into the black.

"So now what?" Mallory asked, quietly. "Now that I know what I 'should have' done? I can't go back and do it over."

"No," he agreed, easily. "That's not how these things work anyway. You have to make amends."

"Oh, is that all?" Her answer was a grin, bright against the night. "And how do I do that, exactly?" Mallory prodded a plastic bouquet with her toe before looking up. "How do I make amends?"

"By apologizing to Head Office, of course."

She gave a bark of a laugh and gestured with her fingers to her ears like a telephone. He laughed back, but genuine, and shook his head. "Oh, of course it's not that easy." The awake part of her mind handed her the answer. "I'll have to go to them, in person, won't I?"

Daniel Gabriel nodded.

She sighed, staring about the cemetery, back towards the crossroads. She had no concept of what time it was, the night could have been three weeks long, it could be ten years from when she boarded the bus bound for Scarborough Town Centre with Aggie, both laden down with presentation cases and relieved that the day was at an end. The moon paused overhead, and even the crickets waited for her answer.

"Okay. Tell me where to go. Let's get this over with."

17.
UPPER MIDDLE MANAGEMENT

As we pulled up to the curb, a fluttering anxiety set in; I wanted to slam down the lock in the door and refuse to get out. The dark of the side street outside the SUV was impenetrable; moths flocked to dance in the headlights, but even the high beams did little to show my surroundings. Daniel Gabriel engaged the handbrake, before leaning back with a breath of impatience and a gesture to the door. "This is where you get out."

I swallowed. The clarity or haze or whatever it was from the dope had cleared on the ride down Yonge Street, leaving me exhausted and confused and sore, although less hungry thanks to Shelly's peanut butter sandwiches and black coffee. "And I have to do this, because...?"

He ran a hand over his face, tired himself, but didn't answer. He gestured at the door again. "You know why. Go on."

I hesitated, my hand over the door handle. I took a deep breath. "Okay. I'm going." I opened the door and stepped out. "Thank you for the ride."

"You're welcome. Remember," Daniel Gabriel called out after me, "just ask. Use your words. Okay?"

"Okay. Thanks again." I closed the door of the SUV and stood on the sidewalk, watching him pull away and turn back into the traffic onto Bloor. Between the lack of signals at intersections and poor visibility and gas shortages—not to mention the sheer time of night—it was surprising to see anyone on the road at all.

I thought of those Humber students, hoping they'd arrived at their new apartment all right. What a way to start your first year away from home...

The tiny street off Sherbourne was old ramshackle houses, details lost to the dark. Everything was dark, no candles in windows like at Bloor and Bathurst. The night had grown a chill, the heat of the afternoon a distant memory.

I crossed the street with careful steps, afraid of broken glass or dog poop in my bare feet. Between two boarding houses stood a small entryway, almost like a shed but with an industrial door. A tiny placard that should have been illegible read:

SHERBOURNE STATION
AUTHORIZED PERSONNEL ONLY

A deep breath for resolve, and I pulled on the handle, half-expecting it to be locked, to resist me. But instead it swung open on easy hinges to a rectangle even blacker than the middle of the night in a power-out.

And yet.

Down in the centre of that gloom was a glimmer. More a feeling or a memory of light than anything vibrant.

I stepped down onto the stairs, and the door swung shut behind me.

*   *   *

The stairs were unfamiliar and I might as well have had my eyes closed. I kept one hand on the handrail beside me, and the other stretched out, my fingertips brushing old, crumbling plaster. Under my feet was cold and slick, linoleum perhaps, except for the safety strip of raised rubber ridges that marked the edge of the riser, because safety first.

And so I descended, the glow never growing closer or lighting the space.

Until it did.

The hallway and ceiling was covered in narrow subway tiles, white once upon a time but grown dingy with age and infrequent washings. The floor was rough poured concrete, but clean enough. Fluorescent lights ran the length of the ceiling, and one flickered and went out before suddenly snapping back on.

I felt like I'd walked this hallway before, perhaps many times, perhaps forever: it seemed as unreal as afternoon. Did it lead to the parking garage? But then why would the gardener have sent me back to Bathurst instead of straight here? Why not just tell me what to do? Why not just—I sighed, remembering Daniel Gabriel's simple advice.

The hallway ended in an opening to an office. There was a counter, and a push-bell. Holding my breath, I rang it. The sound rippled along the walls. If I looked carefully at the uppermost tiles, they seemed distorted, until I realized it was stains from water damage.

I glanced back at the counter and jumped.

The businessman wasn't wearing his pin-stripe suit, instead he had on a maroon TTC blazer, a sweater vest and tie over his button-up shirt. The tie had a shiny pin, like a weird golden W. The vest had a button that said "Ask Me About Transit City!" The face had an expression carved out of stone.

My mouth grew dry, my hands clammy, like I stood in front of the principal, caught smoking. I half wanted to explain that I was in fact in my early thirties and there had been some sort of mistake, I wasn't in high school any more. "Hi."

Not a great opening, I admit, but necessary to clear the blockage between my brain and my throat. "I'm here about a..." Embargo? Lost metropass? Why was I here? He stared at me like I was a murderer or queue-jumper or I'd dinged his Mercedes with my poor-person shopping cart filled with cat treats and single-mother meals. I took shaky breaths and peered around, trying to buy time until I loosened up. "I see you still have lights and power, huh."

His expression didn't change. "This is Head Office." He pronounced it with the capitals. He said it like it was an answer. When I stared back at him blankly for long enough, he clarified: "We always have lights and power."

"No one else does."

"No one else are us."

That was true. And obvious. I drummed my fingers on the countertop nervously and then folded them when his eyes flicked down ever so briefly. Just use my words, huh. That's all it would take, would it? "I want to apologize."

His gaze snapped back to mine like I was a cricket in front of a chameleon.

It took an immense amount of willpower not to fidget or make excuses. "I didn't pay an extra fare to come back after I left the fare-paid area. And I... gave a collector the finger."

Something akin to softening in his features. Now he

was simply annoyed, rather than contemptuous.

"I went outside to make a phone call. And then realized I'd lost my wallet back by the buses. Metropass too."

"There are pay phones inside the fare-paid zones," he answered, testily.

"There were, but they were out of order, and the other ones had this really long wait..." I studied the ceiling. Definitely water damage. Burst pipe recently, perhaps. Unless they'd flooded? "So I am sorry. It was a mistake. I should have explained the situation to someone. I found my wallet, by the way. It was in the trash. Someone emptied it out."

He nodded. That's a thing that happens to lost wallets.

"Just out of curiosity, what would you have preferred I do in that situation?" I asked carefully, casually.

The business man looked thoughtful, then said: "I am sure if you'd explained the situation that the fare-collector would have been able to help you retrieve your wallet and pass."

Most fare-collectors that I'd ever encountered were, at best, bored out of their skulls and certainly not paid enough to care. And let's not forget that Scarborough Town Centre Station was a confusing sea of people asking questions and demanding attention. But sure. Let's grovel a bit if that's what it will take. "Of course. I should have asked for assistance in finding my wallet." From the trash can. "I shall absolutely do that in the future. And again, I am sorry for jumping the turnstile." It was like pulling nails. But if this was the only way to get home...

No. You know what? Screw it. "While we're on the subject of asking for assistance—I'm not sure if you're aware of this, but when I tried to explain the situation to *your* employee, he was insulting—" I laid both hands flat on the counter, "—and then got *physical* with me."

The reward for speaking up was to watch the businessman's eyebrows shoot into the stratosphere. Keeping my voice measured and calm, I continued: "He used some... inappropriate language, and threatened me with violence."

There were several blinks. *Point to Mallory.*

"But this was after you re-entered the fare-paid zone—"

"It is. Does that excuse it?" I smiled. "I would also like to say, in my defence, that I'd already paid the fare when I got on the bus that took me to the station. So you're not even out any money. Because I had a metropass. That was already paid for."

He scowled. Good. Had him on the ropes.

"It's been a long day, for everyone, especially the fine people at the TTC, getting everyone where they need to go with no power and low gas. I just want to get home myself. As I am positive you do too. So what do I need to do to make the embargo end?"

He glared at me for a moment, then stepped sideways and out of view. I tried to crane around the corner of the cut-out but the counter was too deep. So instead I drummed my ragged fingernails on the countertop.

Businessman reappeared. He slid a piece of paper over to me and handed me a pen. Across the sheet were block capitals in Times New Roman.

SPECIAL REQUEST REPLACEMENT METROPASS FORM

Oh, you've got to be kidding me.

*   *   *

I filled out the form as best as I could without being able to look up the details and owing to the fact that it was the middle of the night and I was exhausted. The important things I figured were my address and phone number; I fibbed the rest of the details.

Once I handed the form in, he looked at it and then nodded. He reached below the counter and handed me a temporary metropass, just some official looking card stock, stamped with both the TTC logo and the weird, stylized W from his tie pin.

So that was it. I stared at the card. All that struggle and hassle just because I took a short-cut. What a fucking nightmare. I looked up from the card to the stern, impatient businessman. "Is that it?"

"That's your card, yes. Your official replacement will arrive in about a week."

"No, I mean... the other thing. Is it cancelled?"

He frowned. "I'm sorry?"

I dropped my voice low. "The... you know. The 'embargo'."

"Oh, that." He waved a hand dismissively. "That was cancelled as soon as you apologized. Head Office is very forgiving, if you simply take the time to come in. That's all we ask. Just the courtesy of showing up and apologizing."

I have never wanted to strangle anyone so much in my entire life. Instead I forced the murder down and struggled to smile. "Ah, is that all it takes." Just some simple fucking courtesy, is it? Otherwise we'll hound you to the ends of the fucking Earth or even Mississauga, whichever comes fucking first.

He stood there, waiting.

"Thank you," I said, rubbing a hand over my face. He

turned to disappear back into Head Office; I was done. I could go home. Daniel Gabriel's parting words drifted like lazy-blown smoke rings. "Wait!"

He stopped, expectant.

Feeling every moment of the last few hours like a weight on my shoulders, I asked: "May I use your phone to call a cab, please?"

I rested my head against the cold glass of the window. The occasional headlights of a car going east would drift across my face, but there were few of those, far fewer than even the time of night might lead me to expect.

The time glowed LCD-blue-green in the darkened interior of the taxi, on the edge of my peripheral vision. 3:58 a.m.

3:59.

I stared out the window into the featureless night, clutching my shoe in my lap. Nestled in it was a dead Nokia and a special-request metropass. Dylan would be asleep; I'd have to wake him up since I had no keys. They were in my purse in the presentation case, in some other taxi, in some other world.

This cab was like an airport limo: a Lincoln town car, spotless on the inside, smelling faintly of cleaning solution and (even more faintly) of lavender. The driver wore gloves; I couldn't see his face. I didn't want to.

I hadn't booked the ride, Head Office had done that for me without a word of complaint, giving me a chit to fill out at the end. Then up an ordinary staircase, lit with ordinary fluorescent lights. I had stepped out onto Bloor with the leaves rustling above me, the night breeze smelling of crushed greenery and that edge of sewage that Toronto always gains in the summer, the merest reminder that we live in a swamp. But at that moment, as the limo pulled up, it almost smelled sweet. It was real, and I was going home.

We pulled up outside the health-food store, and gloved hands handed me a pen. I scribbled the details and noted the time—4:11 a.m.—and then signed it, handing it back. "Thank you, miss," a low, gravelly voice said as the door opened to the sidewalk. "Have a good rest of the night."

"You too," I replied as I carefully tucked the receipt into the toe of my shoe, still not sure why Head Office comped me this ride. Remorse, perhaps? I stepped out and carefully closed the door. The car pulled away, red lights disappearing. I didn't mind the gravelly curb under my bare feet. I was so bone tired that I would have walked over glass to get into my bed.

Well, maybe not glass. Maybe dog poop.

Laughter drifted, faintly, its direction unknowable besides "up". All these stores had apartments above, some two or three storeys of them, all with billowing curtains. Dylan's window still had a candle burning on the sill. A faint glow. That was reckless of him, to go to sleep with a candle still burning—unless—my heart caught in my throat and tears burned at my eyes. He'd waited up for me! He was worried. He'd be awake, maybe I could take a shower, and then he'd be relieved, I could tell him about the day I'd had, the journey I'd taken, the ridiculous sights I'd seen, the things I'd done. He'd understand. Of course he would, he was a caring and understanding person and I'd been wrong to ever doubt him—

The laughter came again, and I knew it was his laughter, from his window.

18.
DYLAN

The party moves into the living room as the mosquitoes get to be too much. There's a lot of laughter over prying up melted candles to bring them inside. The beers are gone, the lamb devoured. The apartment windows keep the apartment from being too hot, but it's still warm, and the couch and chairs are soft and the night long.

One by one people drift home, thanking you for the food and hospitality, offering to do dishes too late, offering to host the next one, promising to keep checks on each other if the blackout continues. It's odd that it takes a minor crisis to learn your neighbours' names.

And then there are just the two of you.

A moth bumps against the screen of the window, desperate to get in and reach the candle flame burning only inches away. You wonder how moths survived if they are that stupid as to be suicidal. But then, candles were not a thing evolution worried much about.

Camila is curled up on the couch across from you. She seems tired, but reluctant to leave. You *are* tired but you don't want to be rude and kick her out. You're hoping she falls asleep so that you can just drape a blanket over her and call it a night without having the conversation that's lurking in the flickering shadows.

"What a day," you say, for lack of anything else, hoping she'll get the hint.

But she just nods and stretches, long limbs, very lean and tanned, and you have to look away because otherwise is to invite The Conversation into the foreground. "I'm sorry Mallory didn't make it back in time for your delicious dinner," she says, in Spanish, yawning. "I'm sure she would have enjoyed it, if she'd known." Each word reinforces the fact that *you* know that Mallory *did* know and didn't come home anyway.

"I'm sure she's okay," you reply. It never really occurred to you that Mallory might be anything other than okay, because what Mallory does—and this is what you really admire about her, for all that she's a smart-ass sometimes—is land on her feet like a cat. With that realization, doubts dispel that she's anywhere other than somewhere she's chosen to be for the night. It hurts a little. And with that twinge of heartache, The Conversation scoots a little closer to be said.

"I am sure she's fine," Camila agrees, her voice low and sleepy. She gives a sigh and snuggles against the sofa. "She's probably staying somewhere for the night."

Heartache snags against your ribs again.

Camila's looking at you again in that way that she does, sideways under her lashes, but she doesn't say anything. You can feel The Conversation's breath against your neck. You're just waiting for Camila to say something like "I don't know what you see in her", or "is she always this selfish?" or perhaps even: "why do you go out with her when you could go out with me?"

Ghostly arms of a dialogue you don't want to have wrap its arms around you, like an overbearing relative.

It's an invasion of your space and you don't want to deal with this right now.

But Camila hasn't said anything; *you* have. It's a conversation with yourself, and you know the answers, and you also know the flaws in those answers. It's not the first time you've had the debate.

Camila shifts slightly, leaning towards you. She's just about to say something, and you tense up, not sure how you're going to respond.

And then there's a knock at the door.

19.
HOME SWEET CAMILA

The hallway's only light is the battery-powered exit sign—flickering an SOS from a dying charge—but I know the hallway like I know each blister on my feet. I could have walked it blindfolded. Three paces across the "lobby" that had the mailboxes. Dodge Mrs. Alderman's bucket of salt for icy steps, still there even in August. Then the stairs. My hand alights on the rail through muscle memory. Then a landing with two doors. Two paces and a second staircase. Sometimes there were bundles of newspapers for recycling on these steps, even though the jackass in 1B had been told numerous times not to do it, that it was a tripping hazard.

But I didn't trip.

The upper hallway had its own window; it was closed, no breeze. The air smelled of old cooking. The 3C on the door sat a little crooked, it had slipped while Mr. Alderman nailed it in, and red exit-light glittered around the edges of the fake bronze.

Do you ever have that feeling where you know everything will change and all you can see are the tiniest of details? The water-stains in the ceiling, the cracks in the plaster. The shoes lined up outside Camila's door, all impractical, like the woman doesn't own a pair of sandals without rhinestones. Who doesn't own just a simple pair of sneakers?

The wood flooring warmed under my torn and bloody feet. The beat of my pulse resounded through my toes, like an echo of a drum. It was past 4:00 a.m. He should be asleep. Maybe I'd been mistaken.

No. I'd heard him laugh.

I knocked, tentatively, the sound muffled, and then the beat in my veins increased and with a flat palm I pounded at the door, deliberate and painfully, the shock travelling along my wrist. "DYLAN!" I called, no longer caring who I woke up. "IT'S ME, I'M HOME, I DON'T HAVE—"

The door opened.

"—keys," I finished, the note dying away, my heart in my throat, a blockage and I couldn't swallow. Dylan stood there surprised, his eyebrows around his hair line until he saw me, really saw me, and then he grinned so broadly I thought I'd cry right then and then. He swept me up, his arms tight around me, warm and snug and I buried my face in his shoulder and my eyes burned.

"I was so worried," he whispered.

I knew he was. I knew he was worried and I regretted every time I had chosen a different path than one that led me to a phone. I squeezed back, the shoe pressing against his shoulder blade, until he twitched and began to pull away.

And then there was a squeak of the couch shifting, that one leg that protests.

So slowly it felt unnatural, I raised myself up on my tip-toes to peep over his shoulder. Camila sat curled on the couch, looking back at me. She wasn't wearing very much, her tanned legs pulled up under her, on *my* couch, in the apartment I share with *my* boyfriend. She met my eyes without a hint of shame or remorse or even surprise.

Dylan pulled me into the apartment so he could close the door and felt me tense because he pulled back, confused. "What's the matter?" As I moved my arm away from his back he saw the shoe, and completely bewildered, looked down. "What the fuck! Look at your feet!"

"Yeah," I replied, still watching Camila, who broke eye contact first to lazily look around the room, twirling a piece of hair around her finger. *Twirling a piece of hair around her finger* like a girl in a music video. "Yeah. Lot of walking. I got blisters. And then my heel broke and I threw the shoe at a family of raccoons."

"You... threw your shoe at a raccoon?"

"At a family of them." I dumped my remaining shoe on the nearby sideboard, not caring which of Dylan's innumerable knickknacks I dislodged. My words came out like coins dropped from a height, clattering on the parquet. "They wanted the pizza that I was picking out of the garbage can."

Dylan froze, his confusion clear across his face, and even Camila looked baffled, but then she often had that expression around me. Like she couldn't believe that Dylan had chosen to be with me instead of her.

The apartment was roasting hot–boiling–even with all the windows open and a cross-breeze. Or maybe it was just me.

"I'm not going to ask why you were picking pizza out of a garbage can," Dylan said, carefully, as though I was trying to trick him. "Are you hungry? I think there are leftovers–"

I swivelled towards him in slow motion. "...leftovers?"

"It was a very delicious dinner," Camila said, from the comfort of *my* couch.

I couldn't breathe, and a drum beat inside my head.

Dylan came up behind me to put his hands on my shoulders, steering me towards the hallway. "Why don't I run you a bath? You look like you need one. Quick bath, rinse off, some food, and then bed." He gently guided me along the hallway a few paces and then I turned to face him.

"What. Is. She. Doing. Here." I demanded, in a low voice, fiercely enough that he backed away.

Taking a moment to recover, he replied in the same low tone. "I was being neighbourly," he explained, patiently. "In case you haven't noticed, there's a blackout and none of the apartments—"

"In case I haven't noticed?" My was voice too loud, even to me, but I was long past caring. "In *case* I haven't *noticed*? I have just taken over twelve hours to get home across the entire *fucking* city, you have no fucking idea what I've been through, and there's only *leftovers* for me and *that woman* is sitting on *my* couch at fucking four o'clock in the fucking morning?"

A mask fell over Dylan's features, like curtains being drawn, and in the dim light of the hallway I could barely see his eyes for the shadows. "I figure you've had a stressful day, which is why I'm going to ignore how you're talking to me right now. Go have a bath, Mallory, you smell like a dumpster, and in the meantime, I will go make you something to eat from *my* fridge, in *my* apartment." He turned on his heel.

I turned on mine. It hurt.

But it was nothing like how my feet hurt when they touched the water. It was only water, nothing in it, just luke-warm tap water, but the pain was blinding. Not that there was much to blind—a faint yellow glow from a battery-powered night light over the sink—but I thought for a moment that I might black out. I gripped the edge of the tub and forced myself to breathe shallowly through the agony until my feet were submerged, and then I followed with the rest of me.

Soap was a problem.

Scrubbed, towelled, and nauseated from the waves of stinging pain, I was applying Polysporin and Band-aids to my feet while sitting on the lidded toilet when the door opened. I jumped, looking up, alarmed, but it was only Dylan thrusting a clean set of clothing at me. I took it from him wordlessly and he closed the door.

He wasn't even denying it, I realized. At no point had he said "it's not what you think, Mal!" or anything even close to that. Instead he nitpicked over who owned the couch, who had bought the refrigerator, like we were roommates bickering over common space. Not to mention the food, since Dylan and I bought groceries together. That's not the point! Especially if we end up getting married—oh god. My special meal. She'd eaten my special meal. The one meant as a proposal and *I* was getting the leftovers.

Unless.

Unless Aggie had been wrong and it hadn't been a proposal dinner but a *break-up* dinner. Nausea swirled around me again, like the floor was falling away and I would tumble down forever. What if he'd been carrying on with Camila *all this time*, and tonight was the night he'd planned to tell me it was over? Because he couldn't face another anniversary as a fraud?

My stomach didn't have anything to bring up, but

bile stung the back of my mouth. I forced myself to breathe through my nose until my insides relaxed. Or at least stopped recoiling, settling into a cramp instead. The hand holding the Polysporin clenched, squirting a long worm of ointment. "Fuck."

First things first: finish with my feet.

Then march into the living room and give that hussy a talking-to.

The loose sundress was cool against my skin, and being free from all the sweat of the past day and a half was a blessing, but I was too far gone to enjoy it. I padded out to the living room on my heels, bandaids up off the floor. Camila was still on the couch, adjusting the spaghetti strap of her teeny tank top; Dylan sat in the arm chair, leaning towards her, resting his arms on his knees, speaking urgently in Spanish.

Despite the warm, close air of the apartment, I felt cold. As I came around the corner, both looked up, Dylan stopping mid-sentence. "Now that I'm back, could you speak in English, please?"

Camila wrinkled her nose at me, just a little bit, looking me up and down. I was in a shapeless, faded sundress that I kept for hot Saturday afternoons out on the patio. It was my comfiest dress, essentially only worn whenever nudity wasn't an option. My hair lay in wet ropes around my face and my feet were a complicated interweaving of Life brand bandages. She wore the aforementioned teeny tank-top with short-shorts and still had on make-up, her hair in fetching curls despite the humidity, all without an extra ounce of fat on her, except where it counted, of course.

Dylan stood. "Feel any better? Still hungry?" he asked, the second question emphasized. "I made you a sandwich."

I padded over to the kitchen island, still prickling hot and cold all over. The sandwich was lunchmeat. The lunchmeat that he didn't eat but I did when I needed to pack a quick bite for work. The lettuce was wilted and the tomato gushed over the edge. The plate had a chip in it. My eyes swept over the rest of the kitchen to the piles of dirty plates and cutlery, dishes and bowls. Apparently they'd eaten everything in the fridge. I checked the metal roaster. There were remains of a bone in there, and a puddle of grease. But my nose told me what the meal had been. "Lamb roast. You made lamb roast."

I had to force my breath through my nose slowly, each hit reminding me. Lamb roast was my favourite. Dylan didn't like it. He had only ever cooked it twice before and both times were apologies—once for having to work through my birthday party and once for breaking my laptop, spilling wine over the keyboard. He hadn't said that the lamb was an apology, of course. But I knew.

I leaned against the counter. And he'd made it again. For my break-up meal. I'd been rushing across the city, trying to come home in time for a break-up apology meal. Each inhale was a slap in the face and I turned away.

Both Dylan and Camila watched in silence from the living room, their eyes wide in the gloom. All the flirtatious 'borrowings'. The hidden phone calls in Spanish. He said it was his brothers, and I had no reason to doubt him, no reason at all. Was it really his brothers? Did they know? Did everyone know but me?

Camila was better looking, she shared his Latino heritage, they probably bonded over things that I couldn't pronounce properly while I was on the other side of the city ignorant and focusing on my career. Was it my fault? Did I neglect him? Why didn't he tell me I was neglecting him?

"Mal?" Dylan said. "Are you okay? You look a little green."

She was still here. Still here at 4:00 a.m. What the ever-loving fuck! Why wouldn't this woman get out of my living room so that my boyfriend could break up with me properly?!

The kitchen tilted and I waited for the dishes to slide to the ground.

Somehow Dylan crossed the space without me noticing because he was suddenly beside me. "You're exhausted," he was saying. "We all are. It's been a long day—" He stopped, confused, as I pulled away from him. He pushed the sandwich towards me. "You probably need to eat."

"You made lamb," I whispered.

"Yes?"

"You hate lamb."

"I'm not fond of it, no, but it's all right, lots of tzatziki and mint. I'm sorry there's none left, there were too many people."

"...what?"

"Dylan was very nice," Camila offered, gesturing towards the patio. "He—all the neighbours, they came here and he made the dinner. Out on the—" She was lost for the word and gestured again to the outside. "Everyone brought a something from their kitchen. It was very fun." She yawned, theatrically, and then stretched. "I should be going."

"You think?"

She stared at me, blinking, and then got to her feet, slipping them into tiny jewelled sandals to walk across a hallway. Dylan waited by the door and she stood on tip-toe to kiss his cheek, saying something in Spanish while he looked embarrassed and let her out, locking the door behind her. All while I glared.

"Mallory," he began, in a very slow, patient voice, "I think that whatever you're thinking, it isn't like that, and we can talk about it tomorrow after a good sleep and some food."

"Food," I retorted, gesturing towards the limp sandwich. "You ate my dinner. Without me."

"You were late," he continued in the same slow manner. "Very late. You said you were going to call, and you didn't–"

"So this is punishment?"

"I didn't say that. I am just explaining." He spread his arms wide, open, just as open as his face, covered in stubble already, dark bags under his eyes. He hadn't slept either.

I held onto the edge of the counter, tears springing to my eyes. "You don't know the day I had."

"I don't," he agreed. "When you didn't call, I figured you were trapped on a shuttle bus coming the long way across town. Maybe you couldn't find a phone. Maybe your cell phone died." The Nokia lay where I'd left it, like a failed talisman. "I assumed you'd come straight here, but I guess you must have–"

"Must have what?" I swallowed, straightening. "Must've what? What do you think I was doing this whole time?"

He still had his arms spread in surrender. "I figured... you were either stuck on a shuttle bus or... you and Aggie and the others had gone for drinks somewhere. To wait out for the power to come back on."

"That's what you thought."

"It's almost 5:00 a.m. You've been gone all night. There was no call. What happened?"

My hands shook, even while I rested them on the counter. Smells overwhelmed the apartment: the lamb grease, onions, the sandwich meat, even a wisp of smoke from one of the guttering candles by the sofa. My throat wanted to close. "I wanted to call you. But I couldn't find a phone. I couldn't find a working phone. They were all... something was wrong with them. Like maybe they'd been a pigeon? There was a business man, he was from Head Office and he kept keeping me from doing anything right, he was following me and it was the same guy, over and over and all I wanted to do was get home and be at home here with you and instead—" my voice cracked and I leaned my forehead against the cool tiled top of the island. "It's five a.m. and you're going to break up with me and I just can't even get the words out right now."

"...what?" Dylan froze, mid-step, then leaned on the counter across from me. "What did you just say?"

"About what? None of it seems real anymore. It didn't seem real then."

"About you breaking up with me?" He sounded more than confused, and I looked up, only an arm's length from him. Hurt was written in block letters across his face. Marker script, like the signs on Honest Ed's. "Where did that come from?"

"*I'm* not breaking up with *you*," I corrected. Another smell cut through the old odours of cooking and candles: a fruit-floral wisp of weed. The moon shone through the whispering leaves as a crow cawed, and the breathless voice in my ear urged me to just *ask*. "Do you want to break up with me?"

Dylan frowned, his forehead creasing like he was trying to solve an equation without a blackboard. "Of course I don't. Why... would you think that?"

My voice came out as a bit of bleat. "Because.

Because you made me a special apology dinner, and then you ate it with that bitch across the hall while I tried to get home."

He covered the distance around the island so swiftly and it was all I could do not to cry. He gently wrapped his arms around me and kissed my temple. "I made you lamb because you liked lamb, and I wanted to do something special for you because I'll miss our anniversary next week." He kissed below my ear. "I didn't invite just Camila but all the neighbours. We ate whatever might spoil. We turned it into a party." He kissed under my cheekbone. "I had no idea you when you'd get home and that you were having such a hard time." He kissed my lips. And after a moment, I kissed him back.

He pulled away, staring down at me, smiling, and brushed some wet hair off my forehead. "Your breath is terrible. Eat something."

I laughed. A half-laugh, half-choke, and I leaned my forehead against his shoulder. "You hate lamb."

"I told you, I don't hate lamb. I don't really like it, but Suzy downstairs said to try it slow-roasted with lots of garlic and mint, Greek-style, and she was right. It wasn't bad." He nuzzled the top of my head. "I'll make it again for you. When the power's back. As for Camila—"

My breath caught.

"—I know you think she's out to snag me or something, but it's not true. She's lonely, her fiancé works—"

"Her fiancé?" I repeated, looking up at him.

He put his hands on either side of my face. "Her fiancé still lives in Ecuador. He's working there while she finishes school. Which you would know if you ever sat and had a conversation with her."

"She doesn't like me."

"She's embarrassed about her English. That's why she's so friendly with me. Because she can speak in Spanish."

"She wears tiny tank tops."

"I don't know if you've met many Ecuadorians, Mal, but they are not afraid to show off skin in tiny tank tops." He rested his chin on my head and I curled into the hug. "There really is nothing to worry about. It's you that I love. Not Camila. Honestly, sometimes I find her a bit annoying. But she's lonely and missing her home and her fiancé and I feel bad for her. That's all."

"Really?"

"Really." He looked down at me again and I looked up and I knew he wasn't lying. I knew when he fibbed with me—his eyes twitched and he had trouble keeping a straight face—and this wasn't it. It was just Dylan being open with me and clearing away the cobwebs. That's all it was; misunderstandings and suspicions fostered without sunshine or fresh air. He smiled, and I smiled back, and he gave me another squeeze. "Now, seriously, eat the goddamn sandwich and brush your teeth and come to bed." He paused. "Maybe you can take the day off tomorrow and tell me everything that happened because it sounds like a lot."

"You have no idea," I assured him, as he let me go and pushed the sandwich towards me. It was warm, and a little soggy, but it was the best goddamn sandwich I've ever eaten in my life.

Dylan went around the apartment, carefully blowing out candles, the scent dissipating until all that was left was the breeze blowing through the windows. There was a glow outside, the first inkling wash of dawn. It really was the next morning; Friday. Chewing thoughtfully, I debated just staying up. I mean, in three hours I'd need to leave for the office.

Normally first thing in the a.m. we'd do a post-presentation meeting to discuss questions we couldn't answer the day before, or where materials needed to be improved. But there was no guarantee the power would be back on or subway service would be resumed. And my manager John was off at his cottage anyway.

A pigeon landed on the patio, near the windowsill. It stared at me with its tilted head and unblinking eyes. I crept forward, and left it balled up bits of damp crust on the white-painted ledge. It pecked at them hesitantly, then with more vigour, while cooing at me, fluffing its wing feathers with a dry rustling sound before flying away.

I decided to take the day off.

I think I deserve it.

20.
DYLAN

The sunshine is bright in the windows when you wake up, creeping towards the bed across the parquet floor. You rub your eyes and yawn and stretch, and then roll over; the other side of the bed is empty, and from the feel of the sheets, has been for a while.

You get up. Mallory's clothes from yesterday are still in a pile in the bathroom; you step over and around them to pee and brush your teeth.

As you turn the corner to the living room, you're greeted with that greatest of smells: fresh coffee. Mallory's at the stove, just pouring the heated kettle into the french press. "Morning," she says, cheerfully. She's still in her Sunday morning sundress, her hair in bedhead peaks and demented curls, oddly adorable. She holds up the kettle. "I officially agree that having a gas stove is a good thing in case of a power out."

You have your coffee on the patio, also part of the Sunday morning routine. But it isn't Sunday, it's Friday, and it's eleven a.m., and you call your boss from the kitchen landline but there's no answer and no voicemail.

Mallory leans back against the patio table, her poor feet up on the wooden railing, soaking in the sunshine and fresh air. She looks like she's had to walk over glass. But she smiles when she sees you leaning against the doorjamb, and stretches out arms for you to join her.

"I'm really, really sorry I missed our dinner last night," she says, taking a sip of her coffee as you sit down beside her. "And all the festivities. And made you worry."

She didn't make you worry, she made you frustrated, but that's not worth debating. Instead you put an arm around her and give her a kiss. It's enough that she's apologizing. "I'm sorry you had such a miserable time yesterday. I can make lamb another time."

She sighs. "It's okay, I know you don't like it."

But you smile. "It's good with the right sauce."

She looks at you quizzically. "Yeah?"

"Yeah."

She hmms thoughtfully, taking another sip, and wincing. There's no milk, it's too bitter for her, but she still drinks it. She sighs. "And I'm sorry that I accused you of fooling around with Camila."

You weren't expecting that admission; she'd never said it out loud last night, only implied it. You're not sure what to say. Because the truth was, while you sat in that candle-lit living room with your neighbour, you *had* entertained the notion, if only briefly. But now in the bright sunlight, out on your own little patio with the person you love most, you know it was only tiredness and frustration playing with your emotions.

Mallory's waiting for you to say something, but you still don't know what. So you take a bigger sip of coffee, looking at her over the edge of the mug. Something about that makes her smile and she looks away.

"What's so funny?"

"Oh, nothing, really. Or maybe everything." She reaches into her sundress pockets and pulls out what looks like a taxi chit printed in the blue-gray lines of a carbon copy. She hands it to you and you flatten out the wrinkles so you can make out the logo and the tiny print that says:

FLEET FOOT TAXIS
D. G. Fahrenheit, CEO

"Mallory, just use your words."

You look up at her, surprised.

She's grinning behind her own cup of coffee, enjoying the astonishment on your face. "Sometimes," she says, still smirking, "the universe sends you a message that you can't possibly misinterpret."

You still don't know what to say. Eventually what finds its way out of your mouth is a strangled: "What *happened* yesterday?"

"Oh, it's a long story," she replies, breezily, wiggling her bandaged toes. You recognize her tone. She's settling into her storytelling mode, and when she looks at you it's with real affection and love. "But for all that happened, I really do think it has a happy ending."

END.

*A*CKNOWLEDGEMENTS

On August 14, 2003, I was hanging out with my friend Jane. She was teaching me to make pork & leek dumplings when the power went out. We didn't think much of it, and carried on. Once it was apparent power wasn't coming back on any time soon, we cooked the dumplings in pots on her family's backyard barbeque, and traded with some neighbours over the fence. Later that evening, trying to find relief from the sweltering heat, we went for a stroll and wandered into Mel Lastman Square, finding dozens of families picnicking, relaxing, their kids playing in the fountain. I didn't know then that the scene would become a story seed nearly fifteen years later. So thank you, Jane, for both the dumpling recipe and the memories. (Jane is also the one who spied the full moon through the trees and thought the streetlights had come back on. That really happened—as did me not realizing cell phones did not work like landlines did during a power outage. I still have my little Nokia.)

Along the journey from ~~Scarborough to Etobicoke~~ writing to publishing *Blackout Odyssey*, I've had a lot of help: from my community of Rejectarinos, who urged me to keep submitting after the rejections rolled in, to my early beta-readers Claire & Deborah, who dug in deep to the many Toronto references or accompanied me on walks to make sure I remembered the locales I mentioned. There's Erin & Laura, who beta-read and also supplied details, memories, commentary, and allowed me to vent endlessly when publishing got the better of me, and the faces Marc & Liane, who listened to the venting and joined me in shaking fists in publishing's general direction, sending gifs of consolation and/or victory, the sign of True Frands. Alan beta-read, listened patiently, AND helped me make the cover better, so he gets his own line. Thanks to all of you.

Grace & Lydia: beta-readers since we were all teenagers, listening to me typing away on my 386 and model-M. Thank you for keeping me going all these *decades*.

And finally, one big thank you to my cutie, Lilithe Bowman, without whom this novel would not have been possible. Either in time and space to write or slogging through the slush ranks or patience during my endless bouncing between WRITING HIGHS and submitting lows. Lil, you're the best.

Victoria Feistner is a writer, a graphic designer, and an artisan in equal parts, although some of those parts are more equal than others. Writing speculative fiction for over twenty years, and finishing her first novel at age 18, she has been published in *Salt&Syntax*, *Speculative North*, and *GigaNotoSaurus*, among other magazines and anthologies. Victoria spent the '03 blackout cooking pork dumplings on a propane barbeque and wandering North York in search of a cool breeze. She still lives in Toronto with her partner and two ~~jerks~~ cats; more of her work can be found at victoriafeistner.com.